# Friendly
# Fire

*The*

*John*

*Simmons*

*Short*

*Fiction*

*Award*

University of

Iowa Press

Iowa City

Kathryn
Chetkovich

*Friendly*
*Fire*

University of Iowa Press, Iowa City 52242

Printed in the United States of America

http://www.uiowa.edu/~uipress

Printed on acid-free paper


Library of Congress Cataloging-in-Publication Data

Chetkovich, Kathryn, 1958– .

Friendly fire / Kathryn Chetkovich.

p.   cm. — (John Simmons short fiction award)

ISBN 0-87745-643-7 (pbk.)

I. Title.   II. Series.

PS3553.H433F75   1998

813'.54—dc21                                    98-24438


98  99  00  01  02  P  5  4  3  2  1

*for Don*

*always something*


*I wish to God you'd leave me, baby*

*I wish to God you'd stay*

*Life's so different than it is in your dreams*

—TOM WAITS

*Contents*

ACKNOWLEDGMENTS

Stories from this collection, sometimes in
slightly different form, appeared in the
following publications: "Appetites" in
ZYZZYVA; "Damages" in the *Georgia Review*;
"Driving Home" (as "Laws of Motion")
in *Fine Print*; "The Future Tense" in
*Breaking Up Is Hard to Do* (Crossing
Press); "Dreaming before Sleep" in the
*Mississippi Review*; "The World with
My Mother Still in It" in the *Threepenny
Review*; "As Needed" in *Love's Shadow*
(Crossing Press); "All These Gifts" in the
*Missouri Review*; and "My Real Life" in
the *New England Review*.
With thanks to Cottages at Hedgebrook,
Dorland Mountain Arts Colony, the Millay
Colony for the Arts, and Villa Montalvo for
the gift of time and space and to Alice and
Michael Chetkovich for all their help along
the way. Many thanks, too, to Don Beggs,
Alice Boatwright, Eithne Carr, Carol
Chetkovich, Laura Marello, Mary Kay
Martin, Jessica Neely, Aleida Rodríguez,
Alice Sebold, Roz Spafford, Jude Todd, and
the women of the Friday-night group —
Lin Colavin, Frances Hatfield, Candida
Lawrence, Joan McMillan, Maude Meehan,
Claudia Sternbach, Amber Coverdale
Sumrall, Dena Taylor, Ellen Treen, and
Sherrie Tucker.

# Friendly
# Fire

# Magic Acts

Daphne sometimes says her sister, Lila, is the mother she never had. In fact, Daphne and Lila's mother is alive and quick with maternal affection, but Daphne feels more comfortable going to her sister when things go wrong. Their mother displays an eagerness for bad news that can be unnerving. "Oh *no*," she says when the story has barely begun, and while Daphne is still telling her story she can already hear the echo of her mother passing the news on to her friends. Daphne hears which details her mother will fix on, which events will become confused and transformed—"Now, I don't remember if she said it was her friend's brother or her *father* who was bringing the lawsuit"—and she feels herself becoming frustrated. Their mother, who believes in the evolution of the soul over lifetimes, takes the long view. If things are not better next week or next year, they undoubtedly will be the next time around.

Daphne's sister, who believes in the restorative powers of moping and self-pity, knows how to sympathize. When Daphne calls and feels edgy with tears, when just dragging her voice across that unhappy throat is enough to make her cry, Lila says, "Daph? Oh, honey, what is it? Do you want to come up?"

So Daphne is on her way up to the city to spend the weekend with Lila and Gwen. She's been feeling tired lately—even now, at sixty-five miles an hour on the crowded freeway, she feels dangerously close to sleep and has to keep clenching different muscle groups to keep herself awake—and she's looking forward to stretching out on the sunny carpet of Lila's apartment. Lila is that kind of housekeeper, Daphne thinks—you look forward to her floor. When they were younger and shared a room, Lila ran a strip of masking tape down one wall and along the carpet to the door, dividing the room exactly in half. In the week this experiment lasted, the room looked like a before-and-after ad from a women's magazine.

Lila and Gwen have jobs that Daphne doesn't quite understand, jobs it seems you could do only in a city, where there's so much money flying around you just have to build the right sort of net to catch some of it. Lila has a business called Make It Perfect, which helps people plan everything from first dates to New Orleans–style funerals, and Gwen works as an office-efficiency consultant. People tell her they need to know where to put the Xerox machine or the coffee station, and once she's there, they close their office door and complain about their coworkers. "The Xerox machine is the symptom," she says, "but figuring out who to let go is usually the cure."

When Gwen opens the apartment door to Daphne's knock, Daphne thinks again of her pet theory that Gwen has merged sex and efficiency in a wholly marketable way. She's wearing a simple black jumpsuit and wooden sandals with black velvet thongs that look like something worn in countries where people still sleep when they're tired and eat when they're hungry, and her blond hair curls under cooperatively just above her shoulders.

"Baby Daphne's here!" Gwen calls out, holding her arms open for Daphne to step into a hug. Gwen has no family—"unless you count my mother," she always adds, without further explanation—and she has aggressively adopted Lila's. Lila and Daphne's parents, who loved Gwen when they thought she was Lila's friend and blamed her when they learned she was Lila's lover, have now warmed to her again. The string of disastrous men Daphne has brought home over the years has probably helped, as Gwen points out. Gwen's grateful for that, but now that things are going better she keeps trying to get Daphne to find a nice man. "Alcoholics and egomaniacs are fine when you're starting out," she says. "But you don't want to let them become a habit."

"Spencer is neither of those things."

"Spencer is *married*, Daphne. I don't really consider that a step in the right direction."

There's a smell of sage and garlic coming from the kitchen, and Lila appears, wiping her hands on a towel. She's got about a dozen different pieces of clothing on—an undershirt and over that a shirt and vest, a short skirt giving way to tights and eventually socks—all of it gray and green and brown. She looks as though she's been dressed by children, or birds. But the effect is soothing, beautiful actually. She gives Daphne a kiss on the mouth, as always; in the thirty years Daphne has had to get used to this, she never quite has.

Lila offers her a champagne drink, pale gold with a stain of red at the bottom, a tiny alcoholic imitation of the sunset outside. Daphne has an instinctive moment of resistance in reaching for the glass, but then she reminds herself that it won't matter anyway, and she takes a sip before setting it aside. Lila and Gwen sit next to each other on the couch; Daphne stretches out on the flowered carpet, the spot she's been looking forward to, and closes her eyes. In that moment the idea, the wish, that she might just be late falls away. She knows.

"We have news," Gwen says. "Guess."

Daphne pulls herself to her elbows and looks at them, holding hands like children. She feels that familiar stab of love. "You found a nice, handsome, funny single man and you've invited him to dinner."

"Yes, actually, but that's not the news."

"Lila! You didn't, did you?"

"Oh, Daph, he's nobody, just somebody I work with. I mean he's wonderful, that's why we asked him, but he's nothing to get excited about. Unless you like him, I mean."

"God, Lila. He's not a clown, is he? You know I hate clowns." Daphne drops to the floor again and tries to imagine what this handsome funny nobody might look like. As always when she is trying to think of any other man, she imagines Spencer.

"He's a magician," Lila says. "And very sweet."

"In other words, not your type," Gwen puts in. Daphne's eyes are closed again when she feels the toes of Gwen's bare foot nuzzling her ribs. "Daphne, we're trying to break some major news to you here. You want to hear it or not?"

"You're having a baby," Daphne says impulsively, to hear what the words sound like.

And when her sister says, "That's right! You must be psychic!" Daphne feels something deep inside her turning on its axis.

"Well, we're not having a baby yet," Gwen says. "We're going to start *trying*. We're getting into the baby business."

———————

When Daphne first got involved with Spencer, she went through a phase of imagining what it would be like to have a child with him—a perfect creature with his black hair and quick reflexes, her green eyes and knack for Romance languages. But that phase passed, and one day she realized that she didn't want a baby; at best, she wanted to *want* one. It's the virtues of motherhood that she wants: to feel an affinity with women who cheerfully take on the unimaginable task of being responsible for another human being; to feel at ease when her friends offer encouragingly, "Want to hold him?" She wants to have opinions about how long to nurse and whether to let them cry. She wants to go weak at the sight of one sleeping; even the men she knows—fathers—talk about that.

Spencer has two teenage boys, one of whom, Ben, is a student in Daphne's tenth-grade English class. He's built like his father—lean, with big hands—and he has Spencer's habit of flipping a pencil end over end through his fingers when he's thinking; sometimes when Daphne's at the board and her eyes sweep the classroom for signs of life, she sees him doing this, and the idea of Spencer shudders briefly through her nervous system. Ben is a good student, especially for a boy, but he can be careless, and she often finds herself writing "I know you can do better than this" on his compositions.

It was through Ben that Daphne first met Spencer, at parents' night. She had delivered her carefully prepared twenty-minute speech, leaning heavily on phrases like *critical-thinking skills* and *increasingly fluent command of the conventions of English*, trying not to think what an absurd description this was for what actually went on in her class, where she tried to slip commercials for grammar and paragraph structure into class-long arguments about rap and new movies. Spencer came up to her afterwards, and Daphne thought he was going to ask her whether she really thought an in-depth discussion of the latest voyage of the starship *Enterprise* was going to boost his son's SAT scores. But he held out his hand for her to shake and told her that his son liked her class. His wife was very sick, he said, and it meant a lot to him to know that his son had her class to look forward to every day.

They were standing near the door. Out in the hallway, disoriented adults wandered by, checking room numbers against the schedules they held in their hands. Daphne felt a wave of tenderness break over her. She had a moment of loving everything that she could see: these parents, milling from room to room like children on Halloween; the rows of banged-up lockers and the checkerboard linoleum floor; this man with the sick wife whose son actually *liked* her class.

Later they ran into each other outside and stood talking while the parking lot emptied around them. In the darkness Spencer's voice had the softly burred quality of sanded wood. He sounded like a man worn down to whatever was underneath. They faced each other with their arms crossed and eventually backed apart without touching, but when he asked if he could call her sometime, she found herself saying, "Please do."

Daphne is still lying on Lila's floor, her feelings pulsing like a headache, when Sam the magician arrives. He's short, about her height, and he's got either a goatee or a Vandyke, Daphne's not sure which.

Oh God, she thinks, it's going to be a long night. But there's something endearing about what he does when they're introduced, showing her his empty hand and then reaching gently behind her ear to come up with a tiny pink shell.

"Look what I found," he says, presenting it to her.

At dinner Gwen describes the baby project. "We're going with donor insemination," she says, "otherwise known as the turkey-baster method."

"Lila's going to be the bastee," Sam says.

"*You* seem to know a lot about it." Daphne feels suddenly annoyed by Sam's hearty approval.

"For a while we were talking about Sam being the donor," Lila says.

"Then we came to our senses," Sam adds, winking.

Daphne is shocked by what she finds herself thinking: *Him? A short magician?*

"The books say choosing a friend can be risky," Lila says. "So we decided to play it safe."

"By picking a *stranger*?" Daphne says.

"You should see the paperwork on this stuff," Gwen says. "The clinic probably knows more about its donors than most women know about their husbands."

"Some consolation." Daphne suspects she is going to look back on this conversation and wish she had been more gracious.

Fortunately, Sam is there, with an instinct for what's needed. He raises his glass. "I think it's great," he says. "The miracle of birth gets more miraculous all the time. You two are going to make some baby very happy."

Lila has to work the next day, so Daphne rides to the clinic with Gwen. On the way there, Gwen says, "Something about this whole idea bothers you, doesn't it?"

The little red-and-white cooler, packed with dry ice and nestled in the gully between their seats, makes Daphne feel as if they should be going on a picnic, not a serious errand of procreation. She flips the handle absentmindedly back and forth. "If I tell you what it is, will you promise not to tell my sister?" she says.

"No."

Daphne lets out a disappointed sigh. She realizes how much she wants to tell Gwen, to tell somebody. "It's not about you, it's about me," she says.

"That's usually the case, in my experience."

For a while they don't talk, and Daphne watches Gwen weave expertly through the city traffic. Lila once said it was Gwen's driving that sold her: "I thought, 'This is a woman I would trust with my life.'" Lila and Daphne are terrible drivers; they both hit the brake reflexively when the light turns yellow, then punch the accelerator.

"How did you know you wanted this?" Daphne says.

"For a long time I didn't want it. And then something happened, I guess. I just started noticing babies. It was like when you hear a new word for the first time and that week you hear it three different times. It seemed like babies were everywhere. I'd be talking to a client about setting up a better interoffice mail system and all of a sudden I'd find myself thinking *Sean, Jeremy, Heather.* Baby names."

They're stopped at a light and Daphne looks out her window at a man and his dog on the sidewalk, both sitting on a filthy square of pink carpet. On a small piece of cardboard is written "Only Through Your Generosity Do My Dog And I Eat." Daphne is struck by the formality of the message, and, as always, by the presence of the sleeping dog.

There but for the grace of God, she thinks, but she doesn't really believe it. Nothing in her life has ever brought her close enough to the edge that she could begin to imagine what it would be like to fall off. Nevertheless she is struck by the unfairness of it. Sometimes she wishes agents of the government, clean-shaven men in drab suits, would just come to her apartment and take all the things she can't bring herself to give away but feels guilty for owning: her stereo, her exercise bike, her clothes and books and cupboards full of food.

She's feeling nauseated by the time Gwen pulls into the clinic parking lot, so she decides not to go in. Instead she walks the two blocks back to the man and his dog. On the way, she takes three dollar bills out of her purse and puts them in her pocket, so that she won't have to go through her wallet in front of him. She doesn't want him to see the other bills, how much more she could be giving but isn't. Why three dollars? Four seems cumbersome, so close that it might as well be a five-dollar bill; but five dollars is too much, somehow. Five dollars you would remember later, you would miss.

She walks up to them on the corner and bends down to drop the folded bills into a paper coffee cup. The cup is empty except for a dime and nickel lying on the bottom, and she feels suddenly embarrassed to be leaving so much. She finds herself hoping that no one is watching. When the man says, "God bless you," she thanks him and pats the dog's head.

For the drive home, Gwen puts the cooler with its new cargo of three plastic straws on the floor behind the driver's seat and snugs it in place by wrapping her jacket around it.

"Gwen, it's sperm, not nitroglycerin." Daphne can hear an impatience in her voice that she didn't intend.

"I just don't want anything to happen to it," Gwen says, managing to sound both proud and sheepish, already like a new mother.

Daphne watches Gwen settle into her seat and reach for the ignition. She opens her mouth and finally the words that have been cooped up in her head come flying out: "I'm pregnant, I think."

Gwen leans back in her seat. They're strapped in like astronauts, and for a moment Daphne expects them both to just blast off.

In the ten seconds that she could say a number of wrong things, Gwen says nothing. Then she turns toward Daphne as far as the seat belt will allow and says, "Do you want to be?"

Daphne shakes her head and Gwen nods in response. They go on like that too long, until Gwen finally says, "Weird timing, huh?" and Daphne starts to cry.

Gwen doesn't throw herself on Daphne like a blanket, the way Lila would, to smother her unhappiness. Instead, she takes Daphne's left hand and holds it in her right, as though together they were about to cross the world's busiest street. They sit like that for a while, staring out the windshield at the mural painted on the clinic wall: women of all races standing together, some with children and some without, all smiling.

"Are you okay?" Gwen asks finally. When Daphne nods, Gwen gives her hand a squeeze before letting it go to start the car.

On the way home, Daphne looks out the window at the people passing each other on the sidewalk and thinks, distractedly, that it's a picture of inefficiency somehow—each person coming from a place someone else needs to go. "I keep thinking of something I read once about dogs," she says. "About how every dog likes to play the same trick of bringing the stick back to someone other than the person who threw it. The dog thinks that's a great joke, apparently." She glances at Gwen. "I feel like someone brought me Lila's stick."

"I'm not sure what we're talking about here," Gwen says carefully, picking each word out of the air separately, "but these two things don't really have anything to do with each other. They're not connected. You understand that, don't you?"

---

Daphne decides not to tell Lila yet, and Lila doesn't press her about what's wrong but gives her another hearty dinner. On Sunday morning, watching her sister zigzag around the kitchen, Daphne feels a powerful pull to spend the day with the two of them, sprawled horizontally across big, soft chairs and listening to music, pretending they might eventually go out and do something worthwhile. But she knows the only thing worse than going home to an empty apartment on Sunday is going home to it on Sunday night. She can see herself opening her front door and sending her hand out in the dark to scout the wall for the light switch, her overnight bag hanging heavy on her shoulder, and she knows that vacant, lonely moment is worth avoiding.

Daphne watches Lila pack up a loaf of banana bread and a stack of detective novels for her sister to take home. Most of Lila's hair is tied back with what looks like a paisley necktie, and she's dressed in some intermediary stage between night and day that involves a kimono worn over a pair of pants. She looks to Daphne like something in the process of becoming something else, and Daphne sees it all for a moment as it must look to their mother: our long, slow flight heavenward through lifetimes, the altitude we cannot keep ourselves from reaching. She thinks of the things she could not undo without undoing her life, and she hopes that something their mother is fond of saying is right: that being healed does not always require finding the cure.

# Appetites

—————

I had been sleeping on a friend's floor for a week. I was working nights, proofreading at a law firm, so I had the quiet, dusty apartment to myself most of the day. Next door were three children who all seemed to be at the loudest possible age, their voices alive with the sound of killing each other. After I got up, I would wander the empty rooms, looking in the refrigerator, the medicine chest, the mirror. I would put on a CD and not hear a single song. I would turn on the television and walk in the other room.

I sat down on the couch with the free weekly paper and started working my way through the short list of studios. When I satisfied myself there was nothing there I could afford, I moved to the next column over, the depressingly enthusiastic ads for shares.

> *2 wmn seek third for 3-bdrm apt.*
> *Clean, sunny, safe. Hdwd flrs.*

I circled this one.

I got the machine when I called, but halfway into the message a woman broke in with a voice that sounded like an actress playing a normal person on TV. The room had been rented, she told me, but the person who was all lined up to take it had changed her mind and moved in with her boyfriend at the last minute.

I went by that afternoon. I was buzzed in, and when I got to the third floor a door opened to reveal the most attractive woman I had ever seen. She had a look that made you want to take up painting: red hair, green eyes, and incredible pale, freckled skin. She looked like someone whose job, once you're dead, is to introduce you to God.

I would not have thought a woman who looked like that would ever have to advertise for anything, especially not for a roommate.

"Amanda? I'm Faith." She held out her hand. As I took it, I felt myself being pulled out of the leaky lifeboat I had been paddling around in for the last few weeks. I knew that life near this woman, if I could arrange it, would be different and better. I was prepared to give up whatever was asked of me to make that happen.

"Come in, come in," Faith said, with the becoming touch of an eagerness to please. "Let me show you the place."

Carla, the other roommate, appeared from somewhere, and the three of us walked through a series of clean, airy rooms. I hardly looked at them. When we got to the room that would be mine, I tried to show some discriminating interest by taking note of the placement of the outlets.

"Do you have a lot of things to plug in?" Carla asked.

"No, not at all," I said. "But it's nice to have, you know, options."

"Of course it is," Faith said. "Hey, can I get you something to drink? Water? Or I think we may have a beer."

"Water would be great," I said, avoiding the selfish, alcoholic temptation to take the last, possibly nonexistent, beer.

Carla led me back to the living room and motioned me toward one of those big foam couches that you can pick up and carry under one arm. Across from it were a couple of candy-colored director's chairs that sprang like Easter flowers out of the thick green rug. The only piece of furniture in the whole place that could not be moved by a couple of women with a hatchback was a baby grand piano, gleaming like a casket.

Carla saw me looking around. "Do you have a lot of furniture?"

I waved my hand in what I hoped was a pleasantly incomprehensible way. "Oh," I said, "not really. Hardly any, actually. I'm sort of between furniture at the moment."

Faith came in with three tall glasses of water, a slice of lemon floating in each. The ice tinkled cheerfully as she handed the glasses around.

Carla asked if I had a boyfriend or anyone who might be visiting regularly. I had been looking at a print on the wall across from me—a couple of well-dressed men and a naked woman at a picnic—so I said, "Actually, my boyfriend is going to Europe for a while."

"By himself?" Faith said. Her nostrils flexed briefly. She ran a hand up and down her arm.

"He's wanted to go for a long time and I could never afford it, so we kind of compromised," I said. "He's going and I'm moving."

"I've made compromises like that," Carla said, and I took my first real look at her face. We didn't really look alike, but you'd describe us with the same words on a driver's license: brown, brown, corrective lenses.

There was a little more talk about eating habits and schedules and problems we'd had with roommates in the past—the traditional trick question I thought I handled well by saying I'd always had good luck just talking things out.

My eyes kept drifting over to the piano, which seemed to move closer when I looked away.

"That's mine," Carla said finally. "Do you play?"

I thought this might be the bond with her I needed. "Oh, sure," I said. "Well, you know, a little *Für Elise*, a little boogie-woogie. What about you?"

"I was supposed to be a concert pianist," she said. "From the time I was five."

"Parental expectations. Tell me about it." Carla and Faith waited for me to betray some secret to them. "I could never figure out what mine wanted." The inadequacy of this remark hung there while I tried to think of something else. "Boy," I said finally, holding my glass up and rattling the ice cubes, "this water really hits the spot."

Fortunately Carla seemed willing to let it go at that. She stared at the piano's feet, as though she couldn't bring herself to look it in the keys. "When something's that big a part of your life, it's hard to know who you are without it," she said.

Before I could stop it, a home movie appeared on the screen of my mind. I was pulling up at the emergency-room entrance, and the windshield wipers were slapping the rain back and forth. It was Billy's right arm that I'd broken, so I had to walk around the car, across the path of the headlights, and open the door for him. I helped him out, and then I stood there and watched him move lopsidedly toward the building. When he got close, the big doors swung open like a grocery store and invited him in. For all I knew, he was still in there, though I knew he wasn't.

"Amen to that," I said.

Carla looked at me and nodded.

When I got back from work that night, there was a message from Faith. The room was mine if I wanted it.

---

I knew, of course, that there were women for whom men did their little dance. But I had never actually seen it up close before Faith. Men were always giving her things—cabs, drinks, their cards. She seemed to know how to move through the world saying yes. She had a job, doing PR for a local television station, but her real vocation seemed to be reminding others what beauty God hath wrought.

In the world I came from, landlords were not people who cared, but now that I was sharing an apartment with Faith our tub was getting recaulked, we had screens on all the windows, we were not expected to just live with that funny gas smell. In my old world, if you told your landlord that you'd seen signs of mice under the sink and heard something skittering across the floor at night, he would have asked what you thought he looked like, an exterminator? But Wayne, our landlord's son, said he wanted to come by and "have a look at the problem."

I saw him out my bedroom window a few days later, walking toward the building. He had a paper bag with him; he folded over the top of it and clamped it between his teeth while he tucked in his shirt.

As I walked over to the door to let him in, I caught sight of myself in the mirror and thought of something my mother used to say: *You have such a pretty face, it seems a shame not to do more with it.*

"Hey," Wayne said when I opened the door.

"Hey."

He took a deep breath that seemed to signal a combination of relief and disappointment that Faith had not answered the door in a black-lace teddy after all.

"I take it you ladies are having rodent problems," he said, making it sound like an embarrassing feminine condition. He was standing just inside the doorway, passing the paper bag from one hand to the other, looking around the room. He had one of those little beards under his lower lip that gave you the impression that the phone must have rung while he was shaving.

"It's nothing we couldn't have handled on our own," I said. "But as long as you're here. Again."

Just then Faith's bedroom door opened and several million pheromones swarmed into the room. "Wayne, hi," she said. She didn't walk over. She just leaned against the doorframe, arms crossed. Even from the other side of the room I could make out the jut of her collarbone. Her loose pullover was pitched to one side like a ship in a storm. "I think we must be talking rats here," she said. "I'm not kidding, you should hear these guys."

"Not that we know for sure they're *guys*," I put in, idiotically. Wayne stood there, nodding.

Faith stepped over and pointed at the bag. "What's in here? Is that for us?" I could still see the half-moon mark of Wayne's teeth along the top of the fold.

He opened the bag and pulled out a box of poison. "We've had a lot of success with this particular product." He cleared his throat. "In our various properties, I mean."

"Oh, are all your various properties rat-infested?" I asked, but my question died without an answer, because as I was reaching for the box, Faith took Wayne's arm just above the elbow and thanked him for coming. I recognized the gesture when I saw it: how to touch a man who has not touched you first.

A few days later, the three of us were in the bathroom together, arguing about the mice. Carla was taking one of what I thought of as her wartime showers—a lukewarm spray with the water pressure turned low enough to talk over.

I was controlling the conversation with the hair dryer. "Poison is mean and slow," I said. "You know how it works, don't you? They die of thirst." I turned the dryer on, then flipped it off to say something else. "It's like death by potato chips."

"I could think of worse ways to go," Faith said. She was wrapped in a towel, standing on one leg with the other one propped in the sink, shaving. Her long pale leg looked new, and so smooth I couldn't tell where her razor—a small, heavy men's model—had already been and where it was headed. I bent over at the waist and aimed for my roots.

By the time I straightened up, the shower had gone silent. "Traps, then," Carla said from behind the curtain. "And since you're the one who's morally opposed to poison, Amanda, you can set them."

Carla was becoming the big sister I was always glad I never had.

"No way," Faith said. "No fucking way am I waking up to a dead rat."

"We don't know they're rats," I said, though I was certainly no fan of the trap approach, either.

"We don't know they're not."

"Okay. Poison, then," Carla said. She pulled the curtain aside and our eyes met in the mirror. She was a runner, and she had that runner's body that even naked seems somehow dressed. Her joints were the most prominent thing about her.

"I'm sure there's another alternative," I said. I turned and waved the dryer in her direction. "And if you weren't so gung-ho about seeing them eat themselves to death, maybe we could figure out what it is."

Someone had been taking a fork to my peanut butter—the telltale crosshatch of grooves was there whenever I unscrewed the lid—and I was pretty sure it was Carla, whose own refrigerator shelves were dominated by vegetables in plastic bags and fat-free salad dressings.

"Gung-ho?" Faith murmured. She shaved like a blind person, following the path of the razor with her free hand, stroking her own leg.

Carla, still naked, put her hands on her hips, daring me. "Amanda, they are not just going to go away."

"I didn't say they would. I said we should consider all our options."

"You don't care," Carla said. "You'll be out of here the minute Billy gets back." This had been Carla's suspicion since I had first arrived, in a cab, all my stuff in grocery bags.

Next to me Faith switched legs, pulling the right one down from the sink and propping the left one in its place. Suddenly her towel slid apart and I caught a glimpse of her obviously manicured pubic hair. It flashed like a rune, a sign of all we didn't know and would not even guess about each other, and then it was gone.

"You know, this Billy thing," I started to say, but saying the words out loud was a little like going all the way in the lake after you've been standing there up to your knees. You thought you were used to it, but you're not.

And then, for the first time, it occurred to me that even though I had told no one, he might have.

"Oh, Mandy," Faith said, "maybe it's time to just forget about him." She ran her hand down my arm and her touch was cool. "What about that new guy downstairs? He's cute."

"What guy?" I said, but I knew she meant Clark, the lawyer who lived under us. We had run into each other at a local café a few days before and had ended up walking home together, talking about jazz and football—subjects I could fake my way through if the trip was short. "You mean the guy downstairs? I don't think so."

"Amanda, when you were little and your dog died, didn't your parents ever take you to the pound to pick out a new one?"

"Faith, Billy's not dead!" Carla cried out, and for a moment I thought she knew something I didn't.

"He might as well be." Faith swished her razor around in the sink water. "It's not like you've heard from him."

"Since when are you monitoring my mail?"

"Well, *have* you?"

"Never mind," I said.

"Actually," Faith said, "I ran into him the other day and we started talking and I invited him up for dinner sometime."

"You ran into *Billy*?" Of course, I suddenly thought, they would have met, in one of those clubs they both would have gone to. Making conversation at the bar, a fleck of lipstick on her teeth, his arm in a cast.

"How could I run into Billy if he's in Europe somewhere?" Faith gave me a little smile that made me cinch my robe tighter around my waist. "I ran into *Clark*, downstairs by the mailboxes."

"Faith, if you're interested in him, why don't you just *say* so?" I could hear my voice stamping its little foot.

"Say what? God, Mandy, I told you. I was thinking of him for *you*."

"Did it ever occur to you what *he* might be thinking? I doubt it was *Here's an incredibly attractive girl in a short skirt coming on to me, I wonder what her roommate is like*."

"I was *not* wearing a short skirt."

"Never mind."

"Mandy." Faith waited for me to look at her. Her eyes were the color of moss, of sea-washed glass, of the woods in children's books. "You think being pretty is everything. Believe me, it's not."

Carla, who I had forgotten was even in the room, cleared her throat. "Oh, right," she said.

"What?" Faith said.

"Nothing."

In the mirror I watched Carla oil her arms, touching herself the way a nurse would. I recognized something in her then that I wished I hadn't.

Faith rinsed and dried her leg, then straightened and stretched, her shoulder blades lifting like wings. "Nobody go anywhere," she said, and left the room.

Carla's lotion made the intimate, sucking sound of an animal eating. For a moment it was quiet except for that, and then suddenly a burst of sweet, sad piano music jumped through the floor.

"Listen," Faith called from her room. "Isn't that Chopin he's got on?"

It was a mystery to me how she knew some of the things she knew.

"I've always loved this nocturne," Carla said. She went motionless, a coin of lotion in her upturned hand. She was leaning forward, straining to hear.

I sometimes walked by Carla's room at night and saw her reading sheet music in bed, her fingers quivering as her eyes moved down the page. It reminded me of how my father, after he quit smoking, used to sit at his desk holding an unlit cigar.

Just then Faith appeared in a short black beaded dress that was like a question to which her legs were the answer. She stood in the doorway, the music drifting up around her like smoke.

I wish I could say that the envy I felt was no stronger than what I feel around people who can speak Chinese or understand physics. I wish I could say that any man who would love me for looking like that was not a man I wanted to love.

"How nice!" I said. "Going ice-skating?"

"Faith, that is absolutely darling," Carla said. "Can I ask? How much?"

"Oh, I'm not buying it, I'm borrowing it." Until I met Faith it had never occurred to me that you could actually wear something and then return it. "Think of department stores as huge lending libraries," she said to me once. "Does that make it any easier?"

"So, what the hell," Carla said. She had her towel wrapped around her waist like some old man at a sauna, and her nipples pointed inward in a kind of pigeon-toed stance. "Are we inviting him over for dinner, or what?"

---

Clark came for dinner that Saturday night. I made spanakopita, Carla assembled a kind of Mondrian salad, everything cut into same-size cubes, and Faith picked up an extravagant cake from the bakery down the street. She had gotten it practically for free, because whoever'd ordered it hadn't picked it up. WAY TO GO, MARIE! was iced in spidery script across the top.

Clark showed up in a tie, carrying a bottle of champagne and a small wire cage. "From what Faith said the other day, I thought you could use one of these," he said. "It's one of those traps that lets you catch the mouse without killing it."

"That is *so* great!" Faith said.

"Then what do we do with it?" I said.

"Then you take it somewhere and release it."

"Clark, we live in the city," I said. "Where are we going to release it?"

Faith put her hand on my shoulder. "Amanda, mice *love* the city. There's plenty of places they can go."

Clark showed Carla how to set the trap. They loaded it with a hunk of my peanut butter and stuck it in the dark pantry off the kitchen. I popped the champagne and began pouring.

Faith led Clark on a quick tour of the apartment, and Carla and I, champagne glasses in hand, tagged along. It felt like parents' night at boarding school. In Faith's room a scarf was draped over a lamp; necklaces hung over the sides of her dresser mirror. Carla's room looked like it had been decorated by nuns.

I still didn't even have a bedspread, but Clark was clearly raised right. "Nice blanket," he said when he stuck his head into my room.

Long after dinner, we were still at the table, peeling the labels off the champagne and wine bottles and playing with the melted candle wax. Clark worked over the wire champagne top with one of the attachments on his complicated pocketknife.

"There," he said, setting a tiny ice-cream-parlor chair on the table.

"Show us how to do that!" Faith cried.

"Only if you show me something."

One of the things I admired about Faith was that she always gave a man only what he actually asked for. "Watch this," she said, and twisted her napkin a few times until a swan appeared, a little triangle of cloth folded over as the head.

"It takes a woman to pull that off," Clark said.

"How about this?" Carla put her fingers to her mouth and

let out the clearest, loudest whistle I had ever heard. "Can you do that?"

"Mandy," Faith said, "what can you do?"

I looked at them, the women I lived with who hardly knew me and the stranger I wanted to impress. "I was state yo-yo champ when I was a kid," I said. I had no idea where such a lie had come from.

"You never told us that!"

"Oh, the things I haven't told you." And then it occurred to me that I might be able to pass the truth, like a painful kidney stone, through this stream of inconsequential lies. "I can make ink from pyracantha berries. I know the secret to a really excellent pie crust. I could tell you how to get your bearings if you're lost at night."

I felt them looking at me, half-smiling, confused. I was almost home. "I sent a man to the hospital once."

"Well," Faith said, "you're my choice for desert-island companion."

"Was that by accident?" Carla said. "The man, I mean?"

Aren't most things? I had certainly not intended to find another woman's bracelet on the rug by my side of the bed, and I had not expected to sit on that news until a night when Billy and I had both been drinking.

Billy only made things worse that night—first by lying and then by telling the truth. I didn't mean to do what I did, but I must have known that he would not hit me back. After I punched him, he put out his arm to calm me. I felt no fear. I pushed him away and when that did not satisfy me, I reached for him. I took his arm and yanked and twisted it as hard as I could.

"More by mistake than by accident," I said.

Carla nodded. My answer seemed enough for her.

Somehow the conversation moved on, and eventually we all ended up in the green playground of the living room with slices of Marie's cake. Whatever her mysterious accomplishment—job or house or husband or baby—we hoped it would revolutionize her life.

Then, for the first time since I had lived there, without warning or announcement, Carla walked over to her piano. As she got near, she put out her hand to stroke it, like someone steadying a nervous horse. Then she sat down and lifted the lid, exposing the keys. For a while she just sat there looking at them. "This feels strange," she said. I could see that her fingers were trembling, but also that she had forgotten we were even there.

She began to play, finally, a piece of music I had never heard before. It was an achingly delicate song, not so much music as air, silence outlined by a few notes.

It struck me then that Carla had a gift that had brought her pain simply because it was not a bigger gift, and in my woozy, naked state I felt I had found a key—a key I have found again and lost, found and lost, a hundred times since.

We sat there listening to Carla play. In the pantry I heard a trap door fall. A mouse had been caught, alive. It would be our task to find a safe, hospitable place to let it go.

# *Damages*

_____

Roger was driving down the coast with April, a woman who was not his wife, a woman his wife did not even know. It was a surprisingly warm winter day, and they rode with the windows rolled down, the late-afternoon sun slanting brightly across their laps. April clutched her hair in her fist to keep it from blowing all over.

Now that he had abandoned himself to it, Roger was trying not to think about what was going to happen next. He kept telling himself to just relax and go with it, but his hands felt fastened to the steering wheel, and he could not seem to stop talking about his job.

"The secret of sales," he heard himself shouting over the wind, "is appealing to a person's better instincts. Everybody wants to be a better person. It's the great untapped desire of our time."

It seemed like a long time since April had said anything. "Hey, if you think this is fascinating," Roger said, trying to find his own voice again, "you should see my video presentation."

He glanced over at her. She was smiling at him. "This is nice," she said. "I'm glad we're doing this." She had turned sideways on the seat, her back against the door, and now she leaned her head out the window. Her neck looked to Roger like some private thing that was being revealed to him. He reached over her shoulder and pushed the lock down.

Behind them a car rose up and passed recklessly on the narrow road, trailing guitar music. A young man was driving; on the passenger side, a woman leaned forward, peeling her shirt off over her head.

The world seemed to have cracked wide open, the possibilities spilling everywhere.

"I read somewhere," Roger said, suspecting that it was actually something he had seen on television, "that when they asked Einstein what he thought the most important question facing man was, he said, 'Is the universe friendly?'"

"I've heard that," April said. She was sitting up again, holding her hair at bay. "It all comes down to what we mean by friendly, doesn't it?"

---

They had first met in a lunch place downtown. It was raining, and, because California was in the fifth year of a drought, everyone standing in line was giddy and talkative. The windows had steamed up, and the restaurant, full of laughter and the smell of soup, seemed to be celebrating the simple virtues of a hot meal among friends.

Roger was sharing a table in the crowded room with a woman who was bent over a thick, serious-looking book. He had wedged his folded newspaper under his plate and begun skimming an article on computers and cancer when he felt someone touch his arm. It was the woman.

"Hey, excuse me," she said softly, not lifting her hand even after she had his attention. "Would you do me a favor?"

Roger had the sudden wish that he had chosen another table. He looked up at the woman's face for the first time and felt momentarily reassured by her bangs and glasses, then unnerved again when she took his left hand in both of hers and leaned toward him across the small table.

"That man who just walked in?" she said. Roger looked across the room at a man in a windbreaker who was studying the specials board. His hands, sunk deep in the jacket's pockets, were thrust forward in a way that suggested a hold-up.

"He keeps bothering me," April said. "Maybe if he sees me with somebody, he'll leave it alone."

"Why don't you just tell him you're not interested?" Roger could feel his hand warming up between hers. He concentrated on holding it still, rigid.

"I did that."

"And he's still bothering you?"

"You married guys don't get out much, do you?" she said.

---

Without ever discussing it, Roger and April started regularly sharing a table for lunch. They talked about their jobs, the news, movies they had each seen with other people; they became friends. After missing a few early opportunities to tell his wife, Roger realized uneasily that April had become a secret. He was careful to make sure that nothing actually worthy of secrecy happened between them, and he was relieved when she did not touch him again after that first rainy day. Still, sometimes when making a point she would sweep her hand toward him and he could feel the nerves in his skin being pulled toward her like a tide.

Roger liked to think of his life as a series of fated accidents, each occasion of soberly self-conscious choice prefigured by a chaos of coincidences, drunken whims, missed trains, and the like. He had met his wife, Paula, in a French Lit class he had taken during his junior year. Although his French was poor, he had been attracted to the reading list, and he thought he could manage by sitting in the back and reading the required books in translation.

In class he developed the habit of nodding with his mouth slightly open whenever the teacher spoke and frowning at whatever the other students had to say. One day after class, the woman who sometimes sat next to him followed him out and said, "You don't have the faintest idea what's going on in that class, do you?"

They struck a bargain: she would help him with the papers and he would tutor her in chemistry. The night before the first paper was due, he showed up at her house with a can of coffee and a package of typing paper. She had a table set up in the living room, and while he talked and paced, she typed, spontaneously translating his thoughts—his sentences, his measly little *explications de texte*—into the marvelously incomprehensible French language, with all its gendered nouns and accents going every which way. It was the most incredible thing he had ever seen a person do, and he knew—by the way he was gesticulating and trying to make her laugh, by the outrageous and unlikely references to Chinese philosophy and czarist Russia that he found himself working into his argument, by his persistent wish that he had worn a different shirt—that he was falling for her.

Eight years later, they were still together. And now, by accident, he had met a woman in a luncheonette. When they asked Einstein what he knew, what was it he had said? "Something's moving."

---

On a business trip to Los Angeles, Roger sat on the bed in his motel room and found himself missing not just Paula, whom he always missed when he was away, but also April. On his first day back in town, Roger left for lunch ten minutes early. He walked quickly and caught himself imagining what she might be wearing.

He waited forty-five minutes before he gave in to the possibility that she wasn't coming.

That afternoon, still feeling distracted, he went down the block for a cup of coffee and saw her step out of a drugstore across the street. He had never seen her anywhere but the luncheonette; it took him a moment to recognize her.

"April!" he called out. She looked up and smiled.

Roger crossed the street, jumpy with the feeling that either something was about to happen or something just had.

She was wearing the dark-green dress with the slit in back. Her bangs had gotten too long, and every time she lifted her hand to push them back, a shiny bracelet went sliding from her wrist toward her elbow.

"Look," Roger said. His voice sounded loud, abrupt, the voice that suddenly erupts through everyone else's in a public place. "Do you want to get in the car and go someplace? Go for a drive, I mean?"

"That sounds nice. It's beautiful out."

I know this is code we're speaking, Roger thought. But I'm not sure what the message is. "I'm this way," he said, pointing, as they walked without touching to the car.

---

So here he was, driving south on the coastal highway on a Friday afternoon, April sitting next to him with one leg tucked under her and rifling through his tapes.

After a while they decided to pull off the highway and headed down a road dotted with rickety vegetable stands and drive-in restaurants. Within a mile or so, a block of stores rose up, fronted by a dozen angled parking spaces, and then, as though exhausted by the effort, the town gave out altogether and the road escaped into the hills. Roger pulled the car over and parked. The only building in sight was a church. A man stood on the front steps, checking his watch and looking at the sky.

Churches usually filled Roger with an odd blend of tenderness and disappointment, and this one, white and pointy, was no exception. He had not been inside a church since his sister's wedding, which he thought of now—a dusky, hushed affair after which everyone had stumbled, blinking and disoriented, into the bright afternoon. At the reception Roger had made a sentimental toast, and Paula had danced with his brother. He remembered watching them—his brother's penchant for covering a lot of territory when he danced, the swirl of Paula's flowered skirt as she went gamely along for the ride—and remembered feeling deeply satisfied that two people whom he loved so much liked each other. It seemed to be a message from the universe that he was on the right track.

Mary, his sister, was divorced now, living in a small apartment crowded with most of the furniture from her marriage. She seemed to Roger a person on the verge of being too much or too long alone: the precise fan of magazines on her coffee table gave her living room the quality of a doctor's waiting area, and when she had people over for drinks, she would carry their empty glasses into the kitchen while they were still sitting there. Still, despite the way it had all turned out, Roger remembered her wedding day as a happy one in his own life.

That day, that feeling, seemed precariously far away now. He could sense April next to him, looking out the window and waiting. Her hand, the wild cause of all the trouble in the first place, hung limply over her knee. She cleared her throat and looked toward but not quite at him.

"Well," she said. Roger watched her hand, waiting to see what would happen. When she finally said, "I should probably be getting back," he felt himself break out in a sudden sweat of relief. He had not touched her; he had never touched her, he reminded himself. He had taken a risk to find something out, and now he had his answer.

"Right," he said, nodding. "Me, too."

He pulled back on the road and turned right at the next cross street, heading back in the direction of the highway. But the road didn't go straight through, and after another right turn, and then a left, they were lost in the haphazard streets of a neighborhood.

Roger could feel himself hunching over the steering wheel, his forehead practically touching the windshield. It was getting late. The next turn landed them in the middle of another indistinguishable street, and he watched, feeling more lost than he knew he was, as a woman leaned into the back seat of her car and lifted out a bag of groceries. Behind her the sky was streaked with the hasty, dramatic colors of a winter sunset.

"I think that was it," April said, looking back at the street they had just crossed. "That looked like the way to the highway."

"Thank God," Roger said, pulling sharply into a driveway to turn around. Then, backing out, he turned the wheel too soon and they rolled decisively into a car that was parked on the street.

"Well," April said, sounding annoyed. "So much for a quick getaway."

Roger pulled his car up to the curb, turned off the ignition, and climbed slowly out, expecting to see the porch light blink on and a man come storming down the front steps, pushing up the sleeves of his sweatshirt. When nothing happened, he moved over to the parked car to take a closer look. He could see the dent—a dimple in the fender's otherwise smooth cheek—but there were at least two others, on the door and the rear bumper, and on the whole it looked like the sort of car you see described in the classifieds with the phrase "runs good."

As he was on his way back to his own car, April stepped out and said, "We better tell them. It doesn't look like they heard it."

"You know," he said, making an effort to speak casually, "the damage is so minor, I don't think we even need to bother anybody about it."

April began to walk toward him. Her arms were crossed; she held her elbows in her hands. "Let me see," she said.

Roger stood behind her as she bent over the fender. "Look," he said. "I appreciate your concern. I think it's commendable." He heard himself sounding like a school principal. "But it's my car and it's my decision. I'll take the responsibility."

April turned to face him. "What are you talking about? Taking responsibility is exactly what you're trying *not* to do."

They stood like that for a few minutes, arguing in the quiet street, their voices flaring and dying away like fireflies. Roger became aware of their nearness, the way April slipped one foot in and out of her shoe as they talked. He thought she was just being stubborn; she wanted to make him pay for something, for changing his mind. But she seemed genuinely upset; her voice kept climbing out of reach, calling out from high, squeaky places.

"Shit," she said finally. "I don't care. Do what you want." She plugged her foot back into her shoe and began to walk away.

Roger watched the backs of her knees wink through the slit of her dress. She had given in, and now he wanted to give her something in return. "No," he said. "I'll tell them." She had opened the door and climbed in the car without looking at him, but when he reached across her to get the insurance papers out of the glove compartment, he felt her hand, sweet and tentative, on his back.

As he walked up the path toward the house, he thought of how he and Paula would never have had this argument, and of how her touch would never have moved him in quite this way. Suddenly his wife felt like an old family friend he expected always to love and hoped never to lose touch with, someone with whom you shared the stories of your life—the life that you shared with someone else.

As he stood in front of the door, clearing his throat and lining up his sentences, he heard sounds coming from the house— hoarse, shrieking sounds—and a woman's voice yelling, "Stop it! Stop it!" The long narrow window next to the door had a thickly textured pane, and all Roger could see through it was a dark mass floating, sometimes separating, in a bright field. He heard another shriek, then "No!"

"Oh, Jesus," he whispered. Of course he had to do something; that was the instant, terrifying implication of hearing a woman scream. He stepped back and walked across the yard to where a large slice of light was falling between the drawn curtains of a picture window. In the visible strip of living room, a man was holding a woman from behind, one hand scrambling back and forth across her waist like a small animal. He was tickling her. The woman, flushed and pretty, twisted back and forth, squealing like a child, while a boy in a baseball cap hopped in an excited circle around them.

Perhaps because he was expecting to see something altogether different, the image of a woman laughing in her own living room at dinnertime struck Roger as somehow remarkable. He thought of Paula's laugh, of himself lying on the couch and listening to the waterfall of her laughter when she talked to her sister on the phone. He thought of the way her skin smelled bleached on the days she went swimming, of the way she always said "There you are" when he walked in the door, as though she had just been thinking of him. He loved her.

At that point, the boy took his mother's side and began tickling the man under his arms. "That's it!" the woman yelled. "Get him!" And then she looked up and saw Roger staring at her through the window.

In a moment the porch light was on and the woman was standing at the open door. She was working to catch her breath, and her exhalations made misty puffs in the night air. "Do you *want* something?" she said.

"Oh, hello," Roger said, stepping into the apron of light. "I'm sorry to bother you." The woman looked friendly in an unsmiling way, wiping her forehead against the back of her arm.

It took Roger a moment to remember why he was there. He was still holding the stack of insurance statements and repair receipts, and he held this up and tapped on it lightly with the fingers of his other hand.

"I hope this isn't a bad time," he said. He turned to look back at the car, at April's intent face, and he felt the lie, necessary and honest, come to him.

"I came by this evening to talk to you about why we're here. Why us, why now. Do you ever wonder for what purpose we were put on this Earth?"

"Oh," she said. "Oh, no. We're not interested." By now her husband was behind her, a big man whose curly hair and full beard made an unbroken ring of growth around his face. Roger thought uncomfortably for a moment of the car. "How about you, sir? Have you thought about salvation?"

"Jesus." The man shook his furry head. "Does this approach really work? Do you guys ever actually score any converts this way?"

"We're really not interested," the woman said, inching the door closed as she spoke. "But thank you, anyway. And goodnight, now."

When he reached the car, April leaned over to open the door for him. She was smiling, and her face, tilted and framed in the driver's window, made him feel like he was watching a movie.

"Thank you," she said when he had climbed in. "Thank you for doing that." She spoke in a soft, serious voice. In the dark he noticed her cologne for the first time—a complicated, abstract scent that wouldn't remind you of anything else in the world, not lilies or sea mist, but only the one woman who wore it. He took a deep breath and wondered briefly whether he was being blown off his course or whether this *was* his course. Either way, he knew what was coming, and he did not want to watch: he closed his eyes and kissed her.

# *Driving Home*

It's a fall afternoon in 1969 when Franny has her first clear glimpse of the future. She's twelve, and she's cold. Her hands are jammed deep in her pants pockets, and she's winging her elbows forward and back to keep warm. She's waiting for her mother to pick her up at school and, as usual, her mother is taking forever.

Twenty-six cars have driven by the school by the time the Oldsmobile finally turns in. Franny tugs on the heavy door and climbs in with her books and gym clothes. Her mother looks harried, as though she's been fifteen minutes late all day. They moved to Connecticut six months ago, and she still gets nervous about finding her way; she's always looking in the rearview mirror to make sure of where she's just been.

They come to a full stop at the other end of the circular driveway, and Franny's mother looks both ways on the empty street. On the sidewalk in front of the school, someone's drawn a bunch of peace signs in colored chalk. "Look," Franny says, but her mother's response is noncommittal: "Yes, I saw those on the way in."

"So," her mother says. "How was school?"

"Okay." The diamonds of the chain-link fence are starting to blur past. "I talked to that guy again at lunch. Scott."

"Really?" Her mother sounds pleased and apprehensive. "What did you two talk about?"

"Nothing." Lately Franny wants her mother to know things without having to tell her what they are. Every time she starts to say something, she wants the conversation to be over. "I got Vasco da Gama for geography."

The car creeps toward a green light.

"I hope you weren't mean to that boy."

"It doesn't matter. He's a jerk."

"Oh, Franny, I'm sure he's—*look* at that, would you." A Mustang darts through the traffic ahead of them like a shiny fish. "An accident looking for a place to happen."

"So, Vasco da Gama," Franny says.

"Yes. That should be interesting."

"You've heard of him?"

"For heaven's sake, Franny. I did go to *school.*"

Franny looks over at her mother's pliant profile, her shampoo-and-set hair, and she has a sudden, mean moment of wondering how much her mother really knows about anything—history, science, the war.

"He discovered Florida, of course," Franny says, her voice going bossy with the lie. "He was looking for the Fountain of Youth."

"Uh-huh, I know."

Franny sits there in miserable triumph, pushing the window switch back and forth.

"Sweetie, please don't do that. You'll break it." Her mother clears her throat. "I got a call from Mrs. Bender today," she says evenly. "Doug's mother."

"Oh?" This is a response Franny has picked up at home, her mother's way of answering her father when he announces that he's going out of town on business. "How is she?" Franny crosses her legs.

"Don't do that, Franny," her mother says, suddenly angry. "You know what I'm talking about."

Doug is a wiry blond kid a grade behind Franny in school. He's always talking about what kind of car his father is going to buy him for his sixteenth birthday and how his stepmother was the runner-up for Miss North Carolina a thousand years ago, how she rode down the main street of town waving at everybody from the back of a convertible. Yesterday morning at the bus stop, Franny had picked a fight with him, calling him a name her brother had thrown at their father the night before.

"I *fought* the fascists," their father had responded, his voice filling the room, "which is more than *you* seem willing to do." They had all been at dinner and Franny was suddenly aware of the food in her mouth. "Never mind," her brother said, staring down at his plate. "I'll be gone soon, anyway. I'll be out of your house."

Doug had shown up at the bus stop waving a letter from his brother, who had just gotten to Vietnam. He was ready to "see some action," Doug kept saying; he was ready to "get the job done." Franny could feel her blood suddenly start to charge through her body with nowhere to go, and she went over to him. "You're just a fascist," she said, poking him in the shoulder, "and your brother's a baby-killer!" Then she pushed him with the flat of her hand and knocked his books from his arms. The letter fell in the mud and he started to cry.

Franny stares at the place where the mat is curling up from the floor of the car, and waits.

"She kept me on the phone for half an hour. She was *very* upset." Franny's mother is holding the steering wheel tightly in her fists, as though she expects someone to try to grab it from her.

Franny wants to say, *Why didn't you just hang up?* but what comes out of her mouth is "It wasn't my fault."

"I don't care whose fault it was. I don't care who started it. I don't care about *any* of that." Her mother's voice is suddenly unraveling, coming loose at the edges, and Franny realizes that her mother might be about to cry right here in the car. "You know it's hard for me here. I'm having a hard time. And now *this*."

At the next stoplight Franny turns to look out the side window, but she can feel her mother unlock her eyes from the road and stare at her. "Franny, that woman is pregnant. Think how you would feel if something were to happen, if she were to lose that baby. Would you want to be responsible for that?"

The car begins moving again, and soon a gas station is rolling past, a pay phone, a man stepping off a curb. But the world on the other side of the window suddenly looks flat and unreal; it's as though they're driving through a color photograph. The catastrophe of the phrase *lose that baby* is exploding in Franny's brain, rearranging the rest of the contents into *before* and *after*. Franny stares at her books, zips and unzips the denim pencil bag her mother made for her to take to school this year. *Baby-killer*, she thinks.

She curls her toes tight into her shoes and rocks her legs from side to side. She can't keep herself from imagining her mother telling her father about this when he gets home. They'll be sitting at the table having a drink before dinner. He'll be tired. "Oh God," he'll say in his tired, strained way. He'll take off his glasses and run his hand like a washcloth over his face. "For crying out loud."

She thinks of her brother, running away.

It's starting to get dark when they pull in at the A & P. "I'll wait here," Franny says. Her mother doesn't offer to leave the keys so she can listen to the radio, and Franny doesn't ask. Once she's alone, the big, quiet car feels like a sleeping, not-quite-friendly animal. Franny wipes her nose on the sleeve of her coat. She checks the glove compartment for gum.

Women are streaming in and out of the grocery store, which is lit up bright as a classroom. In the spaces between the signs advertising rib-eye steaks, bathroom tissue, and russet potatoes, Franny catches occasional glimpses of her mother. At this distance she looks strangely unfamiliar, and Franny realizes with a start that she's never before this moment wondered what her mother does when she's not around.

Her mother emerges from the produce aisle, where all the neatly separated vegetables look like the bright blocks of countries on a map, and gets in line. Her raincoat is buttoned wrong, Franny notices, one side hanging below the other.

While Franny is watching, a tall woman with long, wavy hair and a bright red mouth breaks through the line to take something off the rack near the register, and then plants herself right in front of Franny's mother. Franny waits for her mother to say "Excuse me," for the woman to touch her big smiling mouth apologetically and duck out of line. But her mother doesn't say anything, and the woman sets down her basket, rocks her weight to one hip, and pushes the sleeves of her heavy sweater up to her elbows. Standing behind her, Franny's mother stares absently out the window in Franny's direction.

"Mom," Franny says, out loud.

At last, the grocery doors slide open and her mother walks out, hugging the brown bag with one hand and searching her coat pockets for the keys with the other. It takes a long time for her to reach the car.

When her mother finally opens the door, Franny leans across the seat and calls up to her. "Mom. I just remembered. It wasn't Vasco da Gama, it was Ponce de León. Who discovered Florida." Her mother puts the grocery bag on the seat between them and settles in behind the wheel without saying anything. Franny plunges ahead, reciting the teacher's words. "Vasco da Gama was the first person to sail to India. Thanks to him, the Portuguese empire gained great riches from the spice trade."

Her mother pulls the headlight knob out from the dashboard. A sports car rolls by, inches from the bumper, and she stares after it.

"I hate this goddamned place," she says. The swearword, which Franny did not think her mother even knew, sparks out of the sentence and burns briefly in the air. Her mother noses the front end of the car tentatively back into traffic.

Sitting on her hands on the vinyl seat, Franny works hard to imagine that they're riding in a red convertible with the top down. The radio is blaring. They're wearing big, thick sweaters with the sleeves pushed up, and Franny's mother is laughing so hard she's banging her hand against the steering wheel.

They're running away from home; they're discovering the New World. But even through her fierce imagination Franny can feel that other version—the future—snaking its way toward her: she's a native of her mother's country, and when she's old enough to drive, her mother will teach her, defensively, in this very Oldsmobile.

# *The*
# *Future*
# *Tense*

Tom and I lived together for two years, a relatively long time in the graduate-student world, where lives are shuffled and redealt every fifteen weeks and where a temptingly fresh set of new face cards is introduced to the deck every fall. But we finally broke up about a year ago, when it began to seem as though everything that was going to happen between us had happened.

Driving home one night, we quarreled about a movie we had just seen. I don't now remember even what movie it was or why our disagreement seemed so important, so telling, but I do remember the feeling that our relationship, like one of those collapsible plastic drinking glasses, had reduced itself to this one argument.

Tom was driving, and in the green glow from the dashboard I could see his hands resting in his lap, his fingers hooked loosely around the bottom of the steering wheel. He seemed more weary than anything else. "How come our normal conversations keep turning into fights?" he said finally, and the question, which was a good one, made me so mad I was swept by the sudden, ruthless wish for an accident. I wanted him to lose control of the car and run it off the road; I wanted to stand around in the damp air with my arms crossed, waiting for the police to show up. I wanted that much to blame him for something.

Our break-up was punctuated, like our courtship, by a series of phone calls and dinners out. And there was some of that same awkwardness that marks new relationships: every phone call had an ostensible purpose—"I've been looking for that old Sarah Vaughan tape and I was wondering if you had it" or, stretching it, "I thought you might know the cheapest place to rent a car around here"—and each one always began with the gingerly phrased gambit, "Am I calling at a bad time?"

One night when my new apartment was feeling particularly cramped and poorly lit, I decided to go out to the café at the back of the bookstore, a place where you can get a drink in an atmosphere that doesn't make you feel as though, on top of your other problems, you are probably becoming an alcoholic. As I was circling the new-book table, trailing my finger across the glossy covers and generally trying to look more interested in the life of the mind than in fact I was, I glanced toward the café and spotted Betsy McIntyre, the woman who runs the women's center on campus, sitting at a table with Tom.

I think of Betsy as a serious woman in low-heeled shoes who uses the word *intercourse* when other people would say *have sex*, but she has an ungainly, large-featured beauty that can sneak up on you. And her seriousness is tempered by an unexpectedly rich laugh, a sound that can make you feel clever and loved. I heard that sound now, sailing over the hiss of the coffee machine and the clatter of cups and saucers; and when I looked over I saw Betsy leaning back with her face tipped toward the ceiling, laughing, her feet resting comfortably on the rung of Tom's chair.

"Jenny!" Tom smiled and waved me over in that friendly, unconscious way of his that I had at first loved and later tried to change. "Are you here by yourself? Join us!"

"No, oh no," I said. "I should get going. In fact, someone's waiting for me in the car." I waved, though we were close enough to touch, and began awkwardly backing away. We were several feet apart by the time we called out our final goodbyes and I turned and headed for the door. All the way home, I smarted from the obviousness of the lie, the idea of leaving the motor running and a handsome man riding shotgun while I ran in to buy a book.

---

After Betsy moved in with Tom, the three of us went out to dinner a few times, she and I demonstrating that unearthly zeal women have to please and make nice. The conversation at these meals usually felt like something scripted for a public-radio news hour, but Betsy and I managed to work in a number of conspiratorial jokes at Tom's expense, which he seemed to enjoy and which gave us a jocular version of intimacy. I was always tired by the time I got home, but these seemed to be what my mother would have called "successful" evenings.

Still, I did not react particularly well to the news, several months later, that Tom and Betsy were getting married. I had run into Tom at the grocery store, and when he told me, I suddenly had that feeling you get in dreams when everyone else in the room but you is dressed. I actually had the fleeting fear that the scene was being filmed for some horrible new television program, some weird hybrid of *Divorce Court* and *This Is Your Life*, and I tried to dissociate myself from the pathetic contents of my shopping basket—yogurts and frozen food and a jumbo pack of sugarless gum—while I congratulated Tom. I could hear my own voice, squeaky and remote, like a message being played back on someone's phone machine.

At home that night I poured myself a brandy and made a list, more or less chronological, of all the men I had been involved with and why we had broken up. I had been left, I remembered, for a radio d.j., for a senior in comp lit at Smith, and once for the anonymous "freedom to see other people." For my part, I had once left a man who could not promise that he would not be attracted to other women (I was very young and had a rigid notion of fidelity), and later, a man who could not imagine the day that he would want children. I knew these facts by heart, but looking at them now, I saw they were explanations, not reasons—stories attached to mysterious events after the fact to make sense of them, like myths that explain the coming of winter or the sound of thunder. In fact I had no idea what the "real" reasons were, only that at some point we wanted more and more to be elsewhere when we were together, at some point we gave up talking in that flirtatious language of love, the future tense.

When Tom and I were together, we did talk about marriage a few times, but always as a kind of dare. It had the charged appeal of skydiving, a risky adventure glamorized by the slim, but nevertheless real, statistical possibility of total disaster.

It was only early June but it was already hot, and once I got to the hills, the air blowing through the car window smelled like warm wood, that sad smell of summer vacation. The sidewalks and tidy lawns gradually disappeared, giving way to pickup trucks and barking dogs. I drove slowly over the stretch of road where I had once wished for an accident, then past the gas station with the friendly rottweiler and the house where diapers were always out drying on the line, and then I was there.

Many people were arriving at once, the recently parked cars ticking in the heat. Men stood in the road, tucking in their shirts, while women squeezed out the passenger doors and picked their way like cats through the stones and high weeds at the side of the road. In the driveway, I watched a woman lean against a man's shoulder and shake something out of her shoe. She said something and the man laughed, then pulled her close and kissed the top of her head.

As I stood there, staring and thinking about climbing back into my car and driving away, I felt someone's hands close over my eyes from behind. "Tom?" I said. "Is that you?"

The hands turned my head back and forth. I pried them away and turned to look.

"Stuart," I said. "God, what are *you* doing here?"

Stuart is my former ex, my ex before Tom, my ex-ex, you could say. I like him—he lopes good-naturedly from century to century in his studies, giving one the impression that he is not yet intellectually housebroken, and he rhapsodizes about history in a way that most graduate students would consider unbecomingly naive. But whenever I see him it stuns me to remember that we were once involved, that things were ever passionate and sweaty between us, that I have seen him without his glasses on and watched him yell at his father on the phone.

I was glad to see him now, glad for the company. We walked toward the house together.

People were clustered outside, on the patio and in the yard, and the house was cool and mostly empty. It looked the way rooms look in dreams, somehow recognizable overall yet different in all their particulars: *And then suddenly I was in my house, except that it didn't look like my house and there were other people living there.* In the living room, the shiny easy chair I had made us lug to the basement had been restored to its original spot, like a dog that has finally persevered in the long fight to sleep in the house; and our couch—the one we bought at a flea market to celebrate our moving in together—was now covered with a patchwork quilt that gave the whole room a feeling of nights at home and extended family.

It took me a moment to realize that the older woman sitting there, holding a plastic cup in both hands and smiling absentmindedly, was Tom's mother, Nan.

She saw me and patted the space on the couch next to her.

"Jenny. It's so nice to see you, sweetheart. I didn't know whether . . ."

"You too, Nan. You look great."

"And Betsy? She's . . ." Nan looked at me expectantly.

"Yes, she is," I said, trying to sound definite. "She certainly is." And we smiled widely, untranslatably, at each other.

Stuart was standing in the kitchen with a balding Americanist and a throaty-voiced woman who was writing her dissertation on Sylvia Plath. The Americanist was pointing at Stuart's feet, and the two of them were kidding him about his shoes. Stuart was hamming it up, pretending to be hurt. In many ways, Stuart is at his best when he is pretending.

Behind them, an inconspicuously well-dressed man was rummaging through a kitchen drawer. He was tall and handsome in a way that had nothing to do with his features—one of those men you think is in his forties who turns out to be in his sixties. When he had unearthed a bottle opener, he gave a little cry of "Eureka!" and then looked over at me. "My dear, I don't believe we've met," he said.

In fact, we had. Charles was Tom's advisor and friend, and Tom and I had once had a swordfish dinner and three bottles of wine at his house. The two of them had argued through the meal about the efficacy of civil disobedience, stabbing the air with their forks. I remembered watching them, setting my face in an attitude of listening and letting my mind drift behind it.

While I was deciding how much of this to remind Charles of, I felt a hand fall familiarly on my shoulder from behind. "Of course," Charles said, pointing the arrowhead of the bottle opener at me. "You used to be a friend of Tom's."

Tom looked fine. He looks a little like an outlaw preparing for a court date when he dresses up, but he's a handsome man, with a moustache and bright blue eyes, and the look suits him. Right now his sleeves were turned back above his wrists, but he was wearing a tie and new leather shoes.

"Charles is going to marry us," Tom said.

"That should be fun." This remark felt a little off as I said it, and for a moment no one spoke. "Is this all legal?" I added. I was trying to keep things light, but when Charles reached for his wallet and pulled out his Universal Life Minister card, I suddenly felt like the fire marshal showing up to close the circus down.

"Well," Charles offered gamely, "here's to you both." And he swept Tom and me together with a wave of his bottle. "Here's to history."

There was a line of people waiting to use the bathroom, so I walked down the hallway to the one I knew was in the back, between the study and the bedroom. Out the window I could see the far end of the yard, set up for the ceremony with a canopy woven out of lace, ribbons, and dried flowers. People stood around in knots of three or four, their laughter and cheerful curses floating in through the open window. Most of them were my friends, the same people I would have invited if it had been my wedding, and for a moment I had the strange sensation that I was watching an outtake from my own life, a scene that had been shot and was later scrapped from the film but saved, with the idea that with proper editing it could be used somewhere else.

I had rinsed my face and was pressing it with a towel when I heard Betsy's voice rise angrily from the bedroom, on the other side of the door.

"God *damn* it. I *told* you this would happen."

"What? What's happened?"

In my mind I could see Tom hooking his thumbs in his back pockets, that blameless pose.

"You said he'd be fine."

"He will."

"Jesus, Tom, look at him."

I looked out the bathroom window at Charles. He was standing close to the house, flanked by three of the older, more serious grad students, the bearded ones who always sought out the faculty at parties. One of them was holding the neck of a champagne bottle in his fist, and Charles's beer had been replaced by a whiskey glass. Something about him—maybe the way he had pushed up only one sleeve or the sharp angle at which he held his glass, almost spilling its contents—looked wrong.

Suddenly the door flew open and Betsy was standing there, wearing a pretty, flowered dress, her hair tied neatly back with a blue ribbon. She was crying.

"Oh, hi," I said. I steadied myself by focusing on the towel, refolding it with military precision.

"What are you doing back here?" she said.

"Nothing," I said, irrelevantly. Then I took in some air, what felt like all the air that was left in the room. "Tom is being a jerk," I said, hoping that it was one of those moments when you open your mouth and the right thing flies out. I wanted to feel that my history with Tom gave me permission to talk about him this way to the woman who was about to become his wife. I thought it would put us on the same side.

She just stared at me while I put the towel back on its rack, and I felt my mistake. And then I offered her that lamest of consolations: "You look beautiful."

---

As it turned out, Tom was right about Charles, who is the sort of man who can walk away from the brink of drunkenness the way other men can walk away from a good game on television — with regret, but not with genuine difficulty. The ceremony had the brief, anticlimactic feel that outdoor weddings sometimes have, where, because it is hard to hear and hard to see, you have to fight the feeling that you are standing around waiting for it to be over. I looked over at Nan, who now had an orchid pinned to her dress, and wondered what she was thinking. A feeling came over me that I wouldn't mistake for happiness, but that I was nevertheless happy to feel.

When Charles was finished, Tom and Betsy kissed and someone let out a piercing, taxi-hailing whistle. We all clapped and Stuart nuzzled toward my ear and said, "Well, now that Tom's happily married you can tell me. Wasn't I just a teensy bit better in the sack?"

"Gosh, Stuart," I said, clamping my chin and staring at the ground. "I really don't remember."

We stood around for a while, eating cake and drinking champagne, and Stuart went on in this absurd, flattering way, telling me every nice thing he could ever remember a man saying about me. "Bill Schubert likes the way your shirt hangs down below your sweatshirt at softball practice. Alex told me you have this adorable way of eating your salad with your fingers. As if I didn't know."

"You shouldn't be telling me this," I said. "What else have you heard?"

My friend Adele says weddings have a strange effect on men.

"It's kind of a musical-chairs thing," she says. "Suddenly all the unattached guys are thinking, *There goes another one, I better get moving.*"

When I was getting ready to leave, I noticed Charles sitting by himself in an aluminum-framed lawn chair that had once been mine. Somehow, in the way of such objects of indeterminate value, it had become Tom's without my ever actually giving it to him or deliberately leaving it behind.

Charles looked like the last passenger left on the deck of a cruise ship. His legs were stretched out in front of him, and he was gazing out at something in the middle distance. I walked over and asked him if he needed a ride home. "My dear, that would be paradise," he said, and I held out my hand to help him up.

We waded through our goodbyes and made our way to the car. Charles settled himself into the seat next to me, and the sight of his long body tucked into the small space of my car, his head nearly brushing the roof and his knees pressed against the glove compartment, reminded me again of what it feels like to be with a man. I thought again of the men I had loved or thought I had loved, and the ones I thought had loved me. And this time I thought not of why we had parted but why we had come to-gether: how Tom, who knew more about rock 'n' roll than anyone I had ever met, was always slipping homemade tapes into friends' pockets and tape decks and car stereos, for them to discover later; how Stuart had come up to me in class one day, before I had even learned his last name, and told me I had appeared in his dream the night before, stamping my foot and insisting that he read Thorstein Veblen.

I asked Charles how he was doing. He was breathing next to me in a noisy, drunken way, but when he spoke, the words were sweet and even. "I remember you, now," he said. "You had your hair cut short, then. You were all upset, because you and Tom had passed a bad accident on the road that night."

And then I remembered that Charles was right. But the acci-dent had been mostly cleared by the time we got to it—we saw two mangled cars, the smoky flares, and the crushed glass spread like a layer of rock salt on the road, but the ambulance had al-ready come and gone. It had prompted me to ask Tom what he thought happens when you die, and he said, "I always imagine one of the first things is you go in this room. And all the people you ever slept with are there. Everyone looks just the way they looked when you first realized you were attracted to them, and there's plenty to eat and drink."

"Is this supposed to be heaven or hell?" I said. But what struck me was the idea, the *fact*, that we would each move on to other people. It was realizing that we both knew that would happen, even while we were together, driving to Charles's house for dinner, that had upset me.

"Well, my dear. What about you? Will you promise to love and cherish some man someday, whoever he may be, as long as you both shall live?"

Charles's voice reminded me a little of my father's, and I thought suddenly of the telephone call we ritually have on my birthday. I complain about being another year older, and my father always says, "On the other hand, consider the alternative."

And I turned to Charles and said, "I will."

# Dreaming
# before
# Sleep

It was the middle of the night and Harry was trying to coax himself back to sleep by calculating his net worth. He had been right to unload those oil stocks when he did, and right to move on the multimedia company, even when his female broker had tried to discourage him. It was ironic the way he could not seem to make a false move these days.

He closed his eyes and divided the blackboard of his mind into a left half for the running total and a right half for each calculation of shares multiplied by closing price. Of course it was all an approximation, and once you threw in the total guesswork on the house, you were almost picking a number out of a hat. But it was something to think about in the still center of the night, and the latest research on Alzheimer's said it was important to keep the brain active—although to Harry that seemed the idiotic equivalent of saying if you don't want to forget things, you've just got to remember them.

Next to him Marion was breathing with the enviable evenness of sleep. Harry tried to match his breathing to hers, but he kept getting distracted by the dogtrot rhythm of his own heart. His left foot was getting prickly with pins and needles. It seemed suddenly hot in the room. When he closed his eyes he could see the strong, abnormal cells driving out the tired healthy ones in a kind of hostile takeover.

He reached for his wife's hand.

"Are you awake?" she said, surfacing.

"Yes, I've *been* awake. But you go back to sleep if you can."

"No, I'm awake now. What time is it? Do you want the radio on?"

It calmed Harry to listen to the news, the worse the better. Monumental natural disasters were especially steadying—the hysterical reports of devastation, the drone of helicopters in the background, the slow creep of order as the men and agencies began to arrive. Marion liked the talk shows, but that had always been a difference between them: Harry liked facts and she liked opinions. You could tell her something experts had finally proven after long years of study and her response would be "Imagine devoting your life to that!"

Harry had always been enamored of facts, especially numbers, and had only grown more so in their nearly fifty years of marriage. The disturbing thing was how, as you got older, there was less and less real information to pull around you. It was alarming the first time you heard a doctor use the word *mystery*.

"Harry?" Marion's voice sent up a little flare of panic in the dark. She shook his arm.

"I'm still here," he said.

"I know that," she said with relief.

"I was having this dream," he said. Harry was not by nature a deceptive or even particularly inventive person, but he had gotten in the habit lately of making things up in the middle of the night. "I was giving a speech to a hall full of people, and when I opened my mouth, music came out."

"What kind of music?"

He could feel his wife sharpening into consciousness, her body growing more alert next to his. She had taken a couple of dream-interpretation courses at the community college.

"Something classical. Violins." Harry's own preferences ran to Christmas music and Artie Shaw.

"How wonderful. I'd love to have a dream like that."

"Well," he said, feeling sheepish, "it was kind of disconcerting, actually. I kept trying to say something and the words kept turning into music instead."

"Even better." When Marion got to looking on the bright side there was no stopping her. "Like the angels singing."

"Hardly." Really, she could be maddening. But he liked hearing her release the word *angels* into the dark, her flat-footed Midwestern voice calling them down to earth.

It had always been this way with his wife: the things he loved about her and the things he could not stand were the same. He had always assumed that he was smarter than she was, but her flirtatiously uncommitted relationship with facts left her free to think of things he could not begin to imagine. "I don't learn things very well," he had once heard her tell someone, "I just *know* them."

"I don't mean literally," she said now. She gave a little sigh, as though mere words could not begin to capture what she meant. Harry found himself feeling annoyed and comforted. "What else do you remember?" she asked him.

There was that, at least—it was *his* dream. He tried to think of something. "Well, in the middle of it all, this woman stood up and said that was it, she was leaving, someone had to call her a cab."

"Did she remind you of anyone?"

Harry thought suddenly, inexplicably, of a woman he had had an affair with twenty—no, probably closer to thirty—years before. She wore sundresses, and freckles were sprinkled across her collarbone. Melanoma, he thought now. "She had red hair."

"Like your mother's?"

Harry was caught off-guard by this association, which he had never made before. "Not exactly."

"Close enough. What else?"

He had never told Marion about the woman, whose name he now couldn't remember. For years he had been afraid her name would somehow jump across his lips and betray him, and now it was lost to him.

"She had a dog with her. No"—he corrected himself, covering his tracks—"more like a big cat." She, whoever she was, had had a sad-eyed Saint Bernard, and she doted on it in a way that made Harry uneasy. She would walk into the kitchen to make them a drink and the dog would push up off his elbows and follow her, his nails clicking on the linoleum. Harry had never before this moment realized what an unhappy woman she must have been.

"That sounds like it might be sexual."

Harry could feel his face go suddenly flushed in the dark. Marion was always doing this—walking into his head and having a look around. "Of course not," he said.

The pain suddenly grabbed his side and bit in. He took a short tuck of breath.

"What is it?" Marion said.

"Nothing." He turned on the lamp to find his pills.

---

In the morning, Marion got up to make coffee and Harry lay in bed. It took him a moment to remember what day it was. Every day felt like Sunday now, melancholy with rest and unimportance. But today was Wednesday, and that meant Marion would be leaving early for her healing group, where a dozen of them— including *men*, Harry had learned—put their hands on people who were sick and prayed for them to get better. Harry tried not to think about it. When he felt strong the idea of it embarrassed him, and when he was weak it made him nervous. Harry himself did not believe, and the earnest mention of God always struck him like the unconscious brandishing of a bad habit left over from childhood.

When he got to the kitchen, Marion had already finished her own breakfast and put her place mat away. She set his coffee and a bowl in front of him.

"Cereal?"

"You could make yourself an egg if you want. But I don't have time to make you one right now."

Harry had not made himself an egg in fifty years, which Marion very well knew. "Never mind." He reached for the newspaper.

"Well, I've got to be on my way." He noticed she was already holding her purse. "Will you be okay?"

"I think at ten I might have a heart attack. When did you say you'd be getting home?"

"It depends how many people come." Harry had an image of a bank-style line, a long snake of the halt and the blind between velvet ropes. "Before lunch at the latest. Or maybe one, at the *very* latest. Sometimes Jane gets to talking."

"Just tell her you have an ailing husband at home." He spoke to the paper.

"Jane wrote the book on ailing husbands. She's had two."

It was strange how the men died and the women just went on, playing bridge, making meals for the homeless, talking on the phone. Harry did not look up from his paper when Marion kissed him goodbye on the cheek. She smelled, he noticed, of perfume.

"Don't forget to put in a few good words for me," he said, still not looking at her.

"I will," she said, and he was surprised, alarmed, by her seriousness. "I always do."

---

Marion had been gone a couple of hours when the doorbell rang. Harry was back in his study, sorting through a pile of mail with the congressional noises of C-SPAN rising and falling companionably in the background. The sound of the doorbell startled him. Who could it be on a Wednesday? Probably some friend of hers, dropping something off, and he would have to stand there at the door with her or, worse, ask her in. Why were women forever borrowing and returning things? What was the point of being reasonably well off if you couldn't just buy what you needed and leave everyone else alone?

Harry moved slowly through the house, and the doorbell rang twice more. "All right," he said aloud. "I'm coming."

When he finally got to the door and opened it, he saw his two-year-old grandson standing there, both hands raised over his head to reach the bell, tilted against it with all his weight. "Hey!" Harry said, more sharply than he intended. "You can stop that now. I'm here."

The boy turned uncertainly to his mother, who was standing next to him. Harry could see the surface of his face begin to buckle.

"It's okay, sweetie," Cindy said, reaching down to lift him up. "It's just Grandpa. Hi, Dad."

"Your mother's at church," Harry said.

"I know, but we were out this way and we thought we'd stop by."

"Well, that's very thoughtful." For a moment Harry just stood there with his hand still on the doorknob, but then Matthew pushed past his legs, planting a hand on Harry's thigh as he went by.

"Come in, come in," Harry said, backing away from the doorway. He thought fleetingly, longingly, of his darkened study and the mail he had not yet looked at—the solicitations and catalogs, the newsletters from organizations he didn't remember joining. He looked at his watch and wondered how long his daughter intended to stay.

"How about if I fix us a glass of iced tea?" Cindy said, with a brightness that made Harry tired. "And Mattie, how would you like some juice? Come on, sweetie, this way." She started walking toward the kitchen.

"Well, that would be fine," Harry said. He was still standing near the door. "What time *is* it, anyway?" He looked at his watch again. It seemed early for iced tea.

When he got to the kitchen Cindy was going through the refrigerator and Matthew was walking slowly along the edge of the room, his hand trailing along the surface of the cupboards. He was humming to himself. When he caught sight of Harry he broke into a grin and ran over and thrust his head between Harry's knees, almost knocking him down.

"Careful, sweetie," Cindy said, without pulling her head from the refrigerator.

Matthew took a fistful of Harry's pants in each hand and swayed back and forth. Harry put his hand on the boy's head. He felt a love for this boy unlike any he remembered feeling for his own daughters. Marion was always reminiscing about one thing or another that had happened when the girls were small. The only part of these stories Harry really remembered was Marion telling them before.

Cindy handed Matthew a plastic cup of juice and then stood looking around the room with her hands on her hips. It was a stance Harry recognized as Marion's. "Where do you suppose Mom would keep a tray?" she asked, more to herself than to him.

Harry did not like the insinuation that he didn't know where things were kept in his own kitchen, so he walked purposefully toward what he hoped was a likely cabinet above the stove. Inside was an imposing and precarious-looking stack of trays and plates. The discovery pleased him inordinately.

"Here, I'll get that," Cindy said when she saw him reaching up.

"No, I've got it." But Harry hadn't realized how heavy the pile on top of the one he wanted was. His arm began to tremble and he dropped the stack of them back on the shelf with a clatter. He closed the cabinet door without inspecting the damage. "There," he said, handing the tray to his daughter.

When the tea was made they went outside, and Harry and Cindy sat in woven plastic chairs while Matthew pushed a small wheelbarrow around Harry's yard. Harry had gone overboard with the planting this year, and one end of the yard was a chaos of color. On the other side of the house, rows of potted tomato and pepper plants lined the border of the swimming pool.

Harry watched his grandson. He was collecting sticks and rocks, but only certain ones. He held each one up and examined it, then either threw it to the ground or placed it gently in the plastic wheelbarrow.

He was a handsome little boy who looked like his father, a man who was no longer, as Cindy put it, "part of my life."

Cindy was Harry and Marion's middle daughter, the hard one. The oldest had raised herself—good grades, good job, good husband—and the youngest had never really grown up, but she was still a sweet pleasure to be around, and now she had a husband to look after her, so she was no longer Harry's worry. But Cindy seemed unwilling to either work hard for what she wanted or be happy with what she had. It had always seemed to Harry that she was looking for someone to blame and that, although she never openly accused him, the person she most often settled on was him.

Harry thought of himself as a pessimistic person, but he did not take disappointment and bad news personally, the way his daughter always had. It was exhausting and, considering how hard he and Marion had worked to give them all a good life, irritating. "Lots of girls manage with a lot less," he said to her once. "Your mother was no raving beauty and look how well she's done. Everyone loves her."

"It doesn't make me feel better to hear you running Mom down."

"I am not criticizing your mother, and you know it."

"Whatever."

There had been times when Cindy was a teenager when Harry would feel an unfamiliar gust of fury blow through him. He had never hit her—even when the girls were little, that sort of discipline was rare and in any case had been Marion's job—but once he grabbed her by the fleshy part of her arm and held her so tight that when he released her he could see the white stripes of his fingers against the red of her skin. They were arguing about something and she was about to walk away. Her head was already turned from him and her hair was swinging from side to side when he put out his arm—to stop her, he had thought, to hold her still so he could finish what he was saying. But she had tried to pull away and he had tightened his grip. He had pulled her around and grabbed hold of her other arm and shaken her.

Cindy leaned back in her chair now and closed her eyes. "That sun's incredible, isn't it," she said.

"Yes." For a moment Harry thought he heard Marion's car in the driveway. "Your mother'll be sorry she missed you."

"You want us to go?"

"Of course not. I just know your mother always likes to see you." Harry looked over at his grandson, who was crouched on the ground, studying something. His hands were in fists at his sides. "Matthew," Harry called out. "Why don't you show your grandpa what you've got in that wheelbarrow."

"Okay," Matthew said, without looking up.

"Mattie, come on over here," Cindy said.

"Oh, let him be." Everything suddenly seemed to Harry like too much trouble. It was all exhausting.

"I'll get it," Cindy said. She got up from her chair and started toward the house.

"What?"

"The phone."

Harry listened, but he couldn't hear either the ringing or Cindy's voice after she went inside. He hoped it was not for him, but that was ridiculous—it was never for him. Suddenly he thought of a conversation he had overheard once between Marion and Cindy. He had picked up the phone and discovered that the two of them were already on it, and before he could interrupt to say hello, he heard his daughter say, "If that's the way you feel, I don't see why you don't just leave him." Later Harry had wondered what Marion's response had been, but in that moment he had pressed his finger carefully down on the hook and quietly replaced the phone in its cradle. That night he and Marion had gone out to dinner. At one point she went to the ladies' room and seemed to be gone a long time; but she said nothing that night, and nothing in the days after that. The strangest part to Harry was that if he had not picked up the phone, he never would have guessed that such a conversation had ever taken place.

Harry took another sip of his iced tea and set the glass heavily back on the table. It was not sweet enough. Nothing was ever sweet or salty enough since the chemo. He could ask Cindy to bring him some sugar when she came back, but he would probably have forgotten about it by then.

Those were the two things that angered him most—not being able to remember anything and being tired all the time. What was that joke Marion had told him recently, something about remembering the eggs and forgetting the bacon. What time had she said she'd be back? There was no point *trying* to remember, he'd learned that much. Whatever you'd forgotten was like a cat; you just had to wait for it to come back to you, usually when you were thinking of something else.

He heard Cindy push the screen door open behind him. "That

was—" she started to say, and then "Matthew! Dad! Where's Matthew?"

"What?" Harry said.

"Matthew!" She went running around the side of the house, toward the pool. "Oh God, please, God," Harry heard her say.

Harry was a few steps behind her and heard her cry out "Matthew!" before he saw them both, and saw that the boy was okay, the boy was alive. He had climbed down backwards onto the steps at the shallow end and was standing in water up to his thighs, but he had his hands planted firmly on the concrete edge of the pool.

Cindy ran to him and lifted him out of the water. He had been fine until then, but once he saw his mother he began to cry. She held him to her and rocked him back and forth, her nose pressed into the base of his neck.

Harry stood a few feet away from them and did not know what to do. Finally he stepped forward and put his hand on his daughter's back. He patted her a few times but she seemed not to notice.

Just then Marion appeared at the side of the house. "Well, here everyone is," she sang out. She looked especially competent as she approached, the sun shining off her gray hair, the way she walked swiftly and surely over to them in her tennis shoes.

"We had a little excitement but everything seems to be fine now," Harry said. His legs suddenly felt unsteady.

Cindy turned to her mother. She was crying now. "Oh, Mom," she said. "Did *we* ever almost die?"

"Daily," her mother said. She gave Matthew a loud kiss on his cheek. "But since we're all still alive, how about a grilled cheese sandwich. Come on, little man, I could use your help in the kitchen."

Cindy put her son on the ground and Marion took the boy's hand and the two of them made their small-stepped way to the kitchen. Harry felt his daughter there, waiting for him to say something. The pool looked unbelievably blue, more like an advertisement for a thing than the thing itself. "You know what's funny," he found himself saying, "is I never even learned how to swim. I never in a million years dreamed I'd own a house with a pool."

He did not know how to make it happen, but he wanted his

daughter to ask him things so he could tell her things. She stood next to him with her arms crossed. "God, I'm still shaking," she said.

———

That night Harry and Marion went to the Italian place in their neighborhood for dinner. They each had a vodka tonic, and salads with their entrees, but they were there in time for the Early Bird Special, so the bill, including a generous tip for their regular waitress, was less than thirty dollars. Harry put it on his card.

They drove home the back way and Harry pointed out a house, only slightly larger than theirs and on a smaller lot, that had just sold for well over a million.

"Imagine!" Marion said, but she did not really even look at it as they drove by. She had been in the middle of a story about one of her friends, and he had interrupted her.

It was still light when they pulled in their driveway. Marion pointed the remote control at the garage door and it began its gentle lift. Watching it roll up slowly and noisily, Harry sometimes thought of the time their power had gone out and, even together, they had not been able to lift the door on their own.

They watched an old *Columbo* and got ready for bed. Marion looked older at night, without her glasses or her public face on, the expression that reminded Harry of a hospital volunteer passing out magazines. Her eyes seemed to sit deeper in her face, and her skin was shiny with cold cream. She climbed into bed beside him and kissed him on the lips. "Sweet dreams," she said, then turned amiably away from him. He knew she would be asleep in minutes.

"Marion?"

"Mmmmmm?"

"Did you ever think of leaving me?"

"Daily," she said. She did not turn over.

"Seriously," he said, and the seriousness of his voice made her turn to face him. He noticed that a little clip was holding a lock of hair in a curl at her temple. "I heard Cindy ask you once why you didn't just leave me. I've always wondered what you said."

"Cindy? When, today?"

"No, this was years ago."

"*Years* ago? How on earth would I remember that?"

"It doesn't seem like the sort of conversation you have and then just *forget*." Harry could hear his voice climbing in the dark.

"Sweetie, I honestly don't remember. It probably wasn't even anything. We were probably just talking." She yawned. "I'm sure you talked about leaving *me* from time to time."

"Never. I never did."

"Well, that's because you don't talk to people. I'm sure you *thought* about it."

"I *do* talk to people."

"Well, the main thing is I never *did* it, did I? I'm still here, aren't I?"

Harry did not feel at all sure that that *was* the main thing, but he felt unable to put his finger on what the main thing was.

"I think that's sweet that you would worry about it, though," Marion said. She was still turned toward him, but her eyes were closed.

In another few minutes she was asleep. Harry lay there with his bedside lamp on, but he did not pick up his book, a murder mystery. Across the room was Marion's dressing table, on top of which stood a crowd of fancy perfume bottles and a picture of him in his army uniform. They had not met until after the war, and it struck him now as odd to think that the photograph she had kept on her dresser all these years was one that had been taken before she even knew him.

Thinking of the war made him think of that eight-hundred-page biography of Truman he had been meaning to read, and that made him think of his father, who had always admired Truman, even before Truman became fashionable again. Harry thought of his father's grave, in a little town up north, which Harry had not visited in years. He thought of the bootlegger who had lived at the end of the road, and of the lady across the street who used to beat her son with her shoe, and of his best friend, Jimmy, who hitchhiked to Virginia one summer.

*Virginia.* That was the redhead's name. They had met on the train, Harry remembered now. Kennedy had been shot only a few days before, and the woman was crying. Even now Harry could feel the scratchy-one-way, soft-the-other nap of the train-seat upholstery.

He could see everything in such detail, it was more like television than memory. The way the streetlight shone into the bedroom of their first house. The foldout bed they slept on the year they took the girls to the cabin by the lake. The trout Cindy had caught, then refused to eat. The first time he saw Matthew, asleep in his mother's arms in the hospital.

Harry lay in the dark and watched things he never expected to remember and things he had not thought he had seen the first time around. His mind hopped along its associative path, from the view out his college boardinghouse window to the day their oldest, Judith, left for school, to his own high-school graduation, to a dinner party he and Marion had gone to down the street forty years ago, and the way Ed Lotelli had looked at her when they walked in. Then, without meaning to, Harry thought of his recent visit to the doctor, the way the young man had leaned against the front of his desk, his legs crossed at the ankles and his hands holding the edge of the desktop.

Harry lay there in the dark for a moment, not seeing anything. His heart was beating with an off-kilter rhythm, a crazy pirate with a wooden leg. Marion was asleep beside him, and he didn't want to wake her.

He began at the top, with a little company named Aardvark that had jumped 43 percent in the last two quarters. The big board was scrolling through his mind now, and he could clearly make out each quote, even the fractions, as it sailed by. In the darkness his mind calculated with unearthly speed and precision. It had been a profitable day. He was leaving a lot behind.

# Friendly Fire

We are all women and we meet for dinner once a month, in one of our houses.

At Maryann's, dinner usually means an array of delicatessen cartons opened up like origami flowers, with spoons for stamens. Ruth is a good cook, but the possibility that her husband might come home early from the movie or the game, wherever it is he goes, always seems to have a chastening effect. And after dinner at Nina's—another meal of bright, crunchy vegetables served up on heavy earthen plates—we all drive home virtuous and hungry.

But tonight we are at Janie's, which means our drinks are swaddled in cocktail napkins with randy jokes printed on them, and before we even get to the table we've eaten a meal's worth of puffy appetizers that sear the roof of your mouth. Dinner is one kind of meat stuffed with another.

Janie buys all of her cookbooks at used-book stores, and she has amassed a collection from the sixties, the ones whose covers feature blondes in frosty lipstick and sleeveless dresses bearing platters of red meat. She cooks with the ingredients the rest of us have blacklisted from our kitchens, the ingredients of our youth: cream and real butter, cheese and liqueur and whole eggs. The effect is liberating, bacchanalian. We pick at the hardened crust around the edge of the casserole dish with our fingernails. We lick our knives.

After dessert, which is something on fire, we shove off from the table and sail erratically toward the living-room furniture. Nina, a tiny, precise woman who finds comfort in big accessories, rummages briefly in her enormous purse and dredges a kitchen timer from its depths. "I have something to tell you when this goes off," she says, setting it.

Nina is our queen of statistics. The rest of us let the numbers spill over us, the zeros rolling like marbles, and we're never able to remember later if it was a million or a billion, dollars or deaths or jobs or assaults.

"Oh wait, *wait*," Stephanie says. "I almost forgot to tell you. God." Stephanie is the baby, moving toward thirty with the impossible progress of Zeno's arrow, always advancing and never arriving. None of us can ever remember exactly how old she is. She sits cross-legged in her chair, her full skirt bunched in her lap.

"Yesterday, this guy, this *man*, comes up to me in the parking lot, right? It's the middle of the day, I'm wheeling my cart back to the little cart corral, like you're supposed to and no one ever does, and he comes up and goes, 'I'm in trouble. Can you help me?'"

"You didn't," Maryann says. She slides her long, bare fingers up either side of her long nose, lifting her glasses, and rubs her eyes. "God, Stephie."

"I didn't feel like I could just say no without first finding out what he wanted, so I could at least say no to some particular thing. I felt like I was in one of those experiments you read about in sociology, you know? 'Subject was approached by person claiming to be in trouble and just kept walking.'"

" 'Subject was approached and woke up dead.' Does that sound better?"

From the kitchen there's the sound of the kettle's heavy breathing, and then Janie's voice calling out, "Decaf, everybody?"

A moment later, Nina's timer erupts with a bright, startling ring. "That's been six minutes," she says, looking around the room at each of us in turn. "Every six minutes in this country a woman is raped."

"I believe it," Maryann says.

"You'd believe twice that many," Abby says. "You'll believe anything if it sounds bad enough." Early in their friendship, Abby and Maryann discovered that they'd both been involved with the same man, a bond that seems to have granted them the alarming frankness of family. In fact they look like they could be sisters, Abby just a more compact and better-dressed version of the same blue-eyed, black-haired genes. She's our prettiest one. Tonight she's engulfed in a voluminous blue turtleneck that has the lively and elastic look of clothing worn for the first time.

"Come on, Nina," Ruth, our married one, says. "Do you really think the world would be a different place if women had been in charge for the last twenty-five hundred years?" At the pro-choice demonstration we all went to one weekend it was Ruth who kept reminding the rest of us that some of the anti-abortion fanatics were compassionate and well motivated.

Maryann looks at her. "Are you kidding? You're kidding, right?"

"Yes, honey," Nina says. "I really do."

"You're still married," Maryann says. "I keep forgetting that." Maryann's ex has been on the D.A.'s child-support list for two years.

"*Anyway*," Stephanie says, "I thought this guy was going to ask me for money. But he didn't. I got this confusing story about how his mother had just died—*that day*—and his car was in the shop. He said it was the differential—I remember holding on to that like it was proof of something, that the whole thing couldn't be a lie—and finally he asked me for a ride downtown, to where his *brother* worked, he said."

All of us take the same breath—that swift, deep intake through the nose, the one you take for the kind of pain you can see coming.

"So, I did, and I dropped him off where he said, and everything seemed to be fine." Stephanie winds and unwinds a length of skirt around her hand. "But then—well, you know. I got home and realized my wallet was gone."

"Oh, Stephie."

"You're lucky," Nina says. "You are. That could have been a lot worse."

"Sweetie," Maryann says, "that was an incredibly stupid thing to do."

"Stupid, okay, but what if it had been *true*? What if his mother really *had* just died?" Stephanie waves her wrapped-up hand around. "You can't just go around *assuming* everyone is lying all the time."

Janie sometimes says being with Stephanie is like looking at an old photo album that makes your heart want to break because everybody looks so young and half of them are dead now and you're still alive.

"Of course you can," Maryann says. "Let me tell you something. There are guys who dress up like cops and carry phony badges and drive around the highways at night looking for women with car trouble."

"Jesus, Maryann."

"It's true. You think I'm making this up?"

"I'm not as naive as you think I am," Stephanie says.

"Yes, you are. That's just it. You are." It's hard to tell from the soft, exasperated way Maryann says this whether she thinks it's a virtue or a fault.

"Look," Abby says, "all we're saying is be careful. Nina, you took that class. Show Stephanie something."

"How come I'm always the only one who knows this stuff?" Nina says, but she gets to her feet and slips out of her shoes. In her black tights and little black dress she seems smaller than ever, but the huge silver buckle on her oversized belt looks suddenly, gleamingly, dangerous.

Janie appears from the kitchen with a tray of mugs and tiny glasses and a squat green bottle of cognac. "Are we going to talk about the rotten apples all night?" Her voice has a hostessy lilt, and the doll-size glasses look promisingly festive. "Doesn't anybody know any *nice* men anymore?"

"My neighbor got one of those things that fits in your purse. Those stun things." Ruth reaches for her coffee. "Janie, these mugs are great. But the thing about a weapon is you have to be willing to use it, right? Otherwise it's just something else that can be turned against you."

"Three dollars on sale. Crate and Barrel."

"Well, actually, I met a guy last week," Abby says, looking at the coffee table. No wonder she's wearing new clothes.

Around the room our hearts go hard and soft at the same time, the way they do when someone you love gets something you want.

"You did?" Maryann says. "Were you even going to *tell* me?"

"All right. Stephanie, come at me." Nina's got her feet planted in the deep pile of the carpet in front of us and she's rocking lightly from side to side like a boxer. "Like you mean business."

"I'm telling you now. He *seems* really nice."

"Here I come," Stephanie says, climbing out of her chair. "Who is he? How did you meet him?"

"I met him at work. He's a bike messenger, of all things."

"I always wanted to do that," Stephanie says. "God, he sounds great." She begins moving toward Nina with her hand outstretched, as though they were strangers being introduced at a party.

"Not like that, like this. Like you're going to strangle me." Nina demonstrates, and Stephanie backs up and tries again, lurching cartoonishly forward. In a move that looks romantic at first glance, Nina knocks Stephanie's arms apart and knees her gently to the floor.

"We went out to dinner, and then we went to this play. At intermission he said he had to make a phone call, which I thought was kind of strange."

Nina stands over Stephanie, her arms crossed and her feet snugged against Stephanie's hips.

"Nina, you look like someone," Janie says, pointing at her with the coffeepot. "Who is it?"

"Yul Brynner," Maryann says. "In *The King and I.*"

"Who?" Stephanie says from her trapped spot on the floor.

"The bald guy who died of lung cancer."

"Kojak?"

"Here's another thing," Nina says. "If you need help, don't yell *Rape*. No one will come. Yell *Fire*."

"Fire," Stephanie says, but Nina doesn't move. Then she reaches over and taps Abby on the ankle. "So then what?"

"Oh, well, so then he drove me home, and we had that awful what-happens-next moment in the car, and finally I got out and he waited until I was inside, and then he drove off. But one of the phone messages turned out to be that call he made from the theater. He said he wanted me to know what a nice time he was having, how much he liked being with me."

"Quick," Maryann says. "We're losing air pressure in the cabin here. Give us something to make us feel better."

"Well," Abby says reluctantly. "He might be going to India for a year."

"Oh, honey, I was just kidding," Maryann says with relief.

"Okay." Nina finally reaches down to give Stephanie a hand up. "Now I'll be the man."

We're all in our socks and stockings by now, and the cognac is going down smooth and hot. Janie's sitting on the floor, leaning against Ruth's chair, and Ruth is braiding her hair. Her eyes are closed and she's holding her coffee mug in the cradle of both hands. "In the old days a cigarette would have tasted so great right now," she says dreamily.

"God, yes," Abby says. "A Sherman. If I'd known I was really going to quit I wouldn't have wasted my time smoking Vantages all those years."

"I feel that way about being pre-med," Stephanie says. "All those eight-a.m. science classes."

"And getting married," Janie says. "On the other hand, sometimes I think if I'd never married that jerk I'd still be in love with him. God, what a thought."

"Maybe if you'd never married him he wouldn't *be* a jerk," Stephanie puts in hopefully.

The phone rings and Janie answers it. "No he's not," she says. She holds the phone away from her ear and we can hear, like sounds from a faraway carnival, music and the keening laughter of girls. "No, I don't. You might try Josh's."

"Remember that?" she says, hanging up. "Remember calling

boys on a dare? That was fun, in an excruciating kind of way."

"Now it's just excruciating," Maryann says. In front of her Nina and Stephanie are locked in some sort of lethal embrace. "Now it's headlocks and stun guns."

"Well, violence. That's still the exception, not the rule, thank God," Abby says.

Nina's got Stephanie around the neck and she looks over at us without letting go. "You call every six minutes an exception? I'd hate to see your idea of a rule."

"Oh, Nina," Janie says. "So they've kept us down for centuries. They insult us, they ignore us. Some of them are monsters. What are we supposed to do, not fall in love with them?"

"That would be a start." But it's easier for Nina; she's bisexual.

"Do you really believe that?" Ruth says. "You do, don't you?"

Stephanie finally breaks loose from Nina's hold. "So let's call a boy," she says. "Now that I know how to handle one." Stephanie's always the one agitating for charades or pulling out the Ouija board.

"We could call Abby's yogi-biker friend and leave a message on his machine," Maryann says. "What's his number?"

"No way."

"Okay. A stranger, then." Maryann drops her head to the back of the couch and speaks toward the ceiling.

"Answer me, Nina," Ruth says. "You really do think men are the enemy, don't you?"

"Ruth, who do you think is beating all those women up—other *women*?" Nina says. "It's nothing personal. It's just a fact."

"What bullshit," Ruth says. Ruth swears infrequently enough that she always gets a little moment of respectful silence when she does.

Abby nudges Maryann with her foot. "You do it," she says. Her nose is buried in the nest of her turtleneck collar, muffling her voice. "I dare you."

"I double dare you," Janie says, handing Maryann the phone.

There's that blank moment of uncertainty when no one moves or says anything—a moment we all remember from slumber parties and recess periods spent far from the blacktop and the teacher's whistle—when we each feel something we will later recognize was the last chance before regret, and then, a moment later, the phone book is splayed across Maryann's lap and she's flipping through the fragile pages.

"This is great. The men all give their first names." She closes her eyes, stabs a column with her finger, and dials a number. "Hello, Gerald? Gerald"—she looks back at the book—"Mandroni?" She looks around the room at the rest of us and nods. "Hello. . . . Hello."

Maryann says nothing for a second and then abruptly pushes the disconnect button. She clasps the handset to her chest, where it looks like an enormous brooch, something Nina would wear. "This is harder than it looks," she says. "It's *embarrassing.*"

"I think your mistake was saying hello," Janie says.

"You *guys.*"

"Stephanie's right," Abby says. "This probably isn't a good idea."

"No, wait." Ruth, still agitated, stands and steps over to Maryann. "Let me try."

Ruth takes the phone and walks over to the window with it, punching in a number. Beyond her, constellations of lights are burning in the foothills. She's breathing a little unevenly, and when she says "What are you wearing?" her soft voice sounds surprisingly husky. She repeats the question. A pause, then in a softer voice, "Are you alone?"

Three lights in a row, Orion's belt, glitter smartly near Ruth's elbow. Somewhere a dog is barking.

"I'm looking out the window at a light that I'm imagining is your house. I'm touching myself."

The rest of us are frozen in place, our swallows suddenly loud in our ears, but Nina strides over.

"Yes," Ruth says, then hangs up before Nina can grab the phone.

"Wow," Stephanie says. "Get down."

"That is *not* funny," Nina says.

"For God's sake, Nina, that was Tim," Ruth says. "My *husband.*" The word has the heft of something she could pick up and throw.

"That was *Tim*?" Stephanie says. "Wow. What did he *say*?"

Ruth's expression seems to slip and fall, just for a moment, on its way to meet us. "Nothing. He didn't say anything."

"But when you said 'Yes.'"

"I told you, he didn't say *anything*."

"Oh, Ruthie." Janie puts her arm around Ruth's shoulders. "Just because men are jerks and the rest of us are wishing we could meet one is no reason for you to feel guilty about being happy, sweetie."

Soon we're standing and stretching, moving toward the kitchen with our mugs and glasses. In the midst of this the back door opens and two young men in jean jackets and unlaced athletic shoes walk in. It's Janie's son, Todd, with a friend. Who knows what kind of kids you'd think they were if you didn't know them.

Our hellos chirp and bob, and Todd's uneven voice slides under them like a shovel scraping pavement. Janie offers them something to eat and they smile at each other and shake their heads, then edge along the perimeter of the kitchen toward Todd's room.

We pull on our jackets and begin the round-robin of goodbyes as we make our way toward the door. Janie offers to wrap up leftovers for anyone who'll take them. Nina roots around in her purse for the car keys, her arm plunged in up to the elbow. Stephanie, who rides with Nina, starts wheedling at her to put the top down, even though it's October and chilly.

Outside, Maryann and Abby hang over the open doors of Maryann's old Ford while Nina and Stephanie wrestle with the Fiat's stiff canvas top and rusted hinges. Our voices are like telegrams in the night air. "But we'll talk before then," someone says, and from someone else: "I thought it was wonderful. Everyone else hated it, of course."

Finally Nina starts her car, loud as a motorcycle, and she and Stephanie are off, Stephanie's arms held up against the wind.

Maryann rolls down the window and Abby leans across her lap to say one last thing to Janie before they pull slowly away from the house. The big car moves like an ocean liner, the turn signal blinking conscientiously in the empty road.

Janie kisses Ruth good night and watches as Ruth walks down the path and up the road, out of sight. Then Janie steps back into the house and turns off the porch light. On the way down the hall, she passes Todd's closed door and pauses for a moment, raising her fist to knock, but she changes her mind and walks on, turning off lights as she goes.

Ruth and Janie both live outside the town limits, well beyond the civilizing grid of sidewalks and streetlights, where it's often so dark at night that you can't see your own feet. But Ruth always walks the mile home by herself. She does it the way older people insist on climbing stairs or single people make themselves go to nice restaurants alone: because being afraid to do it is worse than doing it and being afraid.

When she's halfway home, walking in the middle of the dark, quiet road, she suddenly hears the sound of someone else walking toward her. She can't see who it is, but she can tell from the sound of the loose pebbles grinding against the asphalt that they're getting closer to each other. Somehow she knows, she can feel, it's a man. A woman would have said something by now, she thinks, even though she hasn't said anything.

Just as they are about to pass each other, the other person stops. Ruth's heart is pounding hard enough to lift her shirt, and her head is pulsing with the new word *Fire*.

Then she feels the person, the man, step toward her. He calls her name, softly, and it's only then that she realizes, with relief and something else she can't place, who it is.

# The
# World
# with
# My Mother
# Still in It

My parents and I are drinking watery Tom Collinses and talking over the sound of *Sixty Minutes*. Several pills are scattered near the corner of my father's place mat, and he occasionally reaches down to rub his leg, which has been cramping and giving him trouble lately.

My mother, who used to manage sit-down dinners for forty, brings out a bowl of snacks made from various breakfast cereals tossed with seasoning salt. It's a recipe she's clipped from one of the health-and-longevity magazines my father subscribes to in her name.

"Well," my father accuses me, "you look good. How's Steven?"

"He's fine." I told Steven he did not have to come along with me tonight—a test he failed by taking me at my word and stay-ing home to listen to the game on the radio. "You look good, too." I hear myself talking in what Steven calls my Donna Reed voice. "Both of you."

My father tilts his head toward my mother. "She's the one," he says. "The constitution of a horse." He rubs his fingers over his knee in a slow circle.

My mother rolls her eyes. "Oh, I know!" she says. "You'll never guess who we heard from today."

I look from one to the other. My father's attention is back on the television. "Who?"

"Ray!"

"*My* Ray?" My mother has the unnerving habit of keeping in touch with my old boyfriends, and I turn around suddenly, half expecting him to come walking through the swinging kitchen door. When he and Anna got married, Steven and I went to the wedding, but that must be four years ago now, and we've fallen out of touch.

"Wasn't he the one that totaled your car?" My father keeps my exes straight with these Homeric epithets. The two-timing one. The one who always called collect.

"For the millionth time, Dad. That was not his fault. He was rear-ended."

My father waves this information away. "As I recall, he didn't pay you a cent for your troubles."

"Dad, it wasn't his *fault*. Besides, the other person's insurance paid for everything."

"Good thing." My father sniffs and turns back to the television. I look at the clock. I've been here half an hour.

"Anyway," my mother says, "he and his wife just had a baby. We got the announcement in the mail today."

For a moment I have that strange, startled feeling you get when you're staring at the phone and it suddenly rings. "That's great," I hear myself say. "Great."

Steven and I talk about children sometimes, but talking seems to be our version of actually having them. I can't exactly say I want them, but as the youngest in my family, with no children of my own, I do sometimes feel like the caboose, hurtling forward and facing backward, watching the empty track behind me run off and disappear through all that open, dusty landscape.

"Poor Ray. I'm sure he has absolutely no idea," my mother says. My father, with his motto "Expect the worst and you won't be disappointed," is considered the cynic in the family; but it's my mother, that realist, who always puts temporary happiness in a long-term context. "I thought I'd get them something," she says to me now. "Do you want to go in on something with me?"

"She let him walk away from a wrecked car—isn't that enough?" My father, clearly enjoying himself, scoops up a handful of the little cereal pillows.

By eight, dinner is over and the dishes are almost done. One of my parents' regular programs is about to come on, and my father hovers in the kitchen doorway, working a toothpick around in his mouth and glancing at the clock. My mother finishes wiping the counters and says "O-*kay*" with the exhaling satisfaction of someone crossing the last chore off a list. She unties her apron, which she's had on since I arrived, and disappears into the pantry.

My father steps over and pulls a couple of folded twenty-dollar bills from his pocket. "Here," he says, holding them toward me. "For gas."

"Dad, you don't need to do that," I say, but he holds the money there, pointed at my heart, and I take it.

My mother returns with a bag of oatmeal cookies in one hand and a small jar in the other.

"Steven likes these fancy mustards, doesn't he?" she says.

From the front door they watch me walk out to the car. "Tell Steven to come along next time," my mother calls out.

"Not if he's working," my father adds. "You tell him if he has to work, we understand." After the years I spent with film students and drummers between bands, my father still can't quite believe I married a man with a job.

Outside the light is just beginning to fade, and the air is still soft and warm. I drive home with the windows rolled down to let in the summer evening: the smell of watered concrete, chlorine from someone's pool, a sudden sweet blossom my father, an unlikely gardener, would know the name of. I wish for things without knowing what they are.

At home Steven is lying on the couch in the darkening room, listening to the game. His head and feet, in socks that are wearing at the heel, are propped on the arms of the couch. On the radio the Giants' middle reliever gives up a double, and a run scores.

I have trouble for a second recognizing this as the life I have chosen, but then Steven moves over to make room for me on the couch. He takes my hand and asks me how I'm doing.

A walk, then a single, and then the manager takes what announcers always refer to as that long, slow trip to the mound. I can feel the length of Steven's body next to mine. I rest my hand on his thigh.

Soon it's almost completely dark except for the tiny red lights on the stereo receiver. I suddenly remember that it was Ray who taught me the boy's pleasure of listening to a game in the dark, and I later taught it to Steven.

In the darkness Steven's body is a kind of palimpsest on which I can make out the faint erased marks of the few important ones who came before. Ray was the first of these, so he became the prototype for all the handsome preoccupied men I fell in love with after—the ones who, when we were out, would pull me close and kiss me on the forehead while they looked over my head at something down the street.

A year or so after we broke up, I saw Ray at a party that we had both gone to alone. I was still so young that I even thought of myself as young; I remember a feeling I had then, that the cement of my life had not even been poured, much less begun to set. A couple of hours into the party, when I saw Ray go into the bathroom, I slipped in after him.

He hesitated for a moment, then stepped over to the toilet and unzipped his pants. Later that night we ended up back at his apartment and made that familiar, distracted love once more, but it was the ease of sitting on the bathroom counter while he peed, not the sex, that reminded me of my heart by breaking it.

"I've had a hard time getting over you," he said, playing with my hair in the darkness of his bedroom. "I hope to God you don't intend to put us both through that again."

That seems to be my special gift, getting men to throw me the keys on condition that I won't take them anywhere.

"My arm's asleep," Steven says, pulling it from under my neck.

It's the eighth inning, and the game is now comfortably out of reach; it's just a matter of nailing the last pieces of the loss into place.

"Ray and his wife just had a baby," I say into the darkness, and Steven, God love him, says, "Ray who?"

---

I lock my eyes on the back of my mother's flowered overblouse as we tack our way toward the baby department. I get dizzy and fatigued if I step off the linoleum trail in department stores, but my mother bushwhacks her way through that dense landscape of fabric with her usual sense of direction, empty sleeves swinging in her wake.

"It's not too late for you, you know," she says, shuffling expertly through the tiny outfits on the sale rack. "This is cute"— she checks a price tag—"well, not *that* cute." She moves to another rack.

"Oh, Mom." I squeeze a grunting pig and a quacking duck in conversation. I'm doing what I always do when I go shopping with my mother—waiting for her to make up our mind.

"I'm just talking," she says. "I'm not saying anything."

I've never told my mother about the abortion I had with Ray, and this moment among the pastels and friendly animals at Macy's suddenly seems as close to telling her as I am likely to get. But it's like spotting the exit for a place you've always meant to go while you're on the freeway headed somewhere else.

"He always seemed like a lost soul," my mother says cheerfully. "Maybe fatherhood will bring him back to earth."

We finally settle on a bright-yellow outfit and a cow with big black stitches for eyelashes. On our way back across the store we pull up at a table piled with sweaters and my mother tries to buy me one.

"Or would you rather have something else?" she says, when I look at them without picking one up. "A skirt, maybe?"

I can see where this is going, so I set the shopping bag down to pick up a sweater, and when I reach down again for the handles, the cow's harlequin face is looking up at me from its nest of tissue paper. For a strange, mixed-up moment, I imagine my mother snapping Ray's new daughter into her little yellow playsuit while my father stands a few feet away, making funny noises and congratulating himself on getting the baby to smile.

We buy the sweater and cross the mall to a coffee place my mother likes. After we sit down she leans across the table conspiratorially. "That man over there goes to my church. His wife died last year."

Even sitting down, the man looks unsteady; he stirs his coffee with a badly shaking hand. He looks like someone you would hate to be behind on the road.

"Is he okay?" I say.

"What do you mean?"

I shrug. "He seems old."

"He's younger than your father."

Before we leave, my mother gets up to go to the rest room. On the way, she stops at the old man's table. He starts to get up but she touches his shoulder lightly and he sinks back down. He gestures to the chair across from him, and my mother smiles but gestures back to me. He takes her hand in both of his. If something were to happen to my father, I find myself thinking, this guy would be standing in line. The word *stepfather* jumps incongruously into my mind.

Finally my mother heads down the hallway to the rest rooms and I get up to pay the check. The cashier, a dark-haired beauty, is busy flirting with the young man piloting the espresso machine.

"Excuse me," I say.

"Sure," she says, taking the slip without looking at me. She has rings on six or seven fingers, and her eyes are outlined in black. I feel a brief stab of regret that when I was the age to wear that look myself, I was convinced that makeup and too much jewelry were tools of the patriarchy.

After I pay, I move toward the door to wait for my mother. Outside, in the filtered light of the mall, kids stand around with their arms crossed and women wheel by with their strollers. A few minutes later, when my mother still has not appeared, I turn back toward the tables to look for her.

The old man is gone and there is my mother, standing at the mouth of the hallway, searching the room of tables. When she does not step forward but just stands there, holding her purse in both hands, I realize she's lost.

"Mom! Mom!" I hurry toward her. I can see her start to smile at the sound of my voice. When she spots me, her shoulders drop in relief.

"That was the strangest thing," she says as soon as I reach her, picking the moment up and putting it carefully in the past. "I just got completely turned around when I came out of the ladies' room, I guess."

"Are you okay?"

"Oh yes, I'm fine. You know how that is when everything suddenly looks unfamiliar."

I do not say what I am thinking. Neither does she. I move both shopping bags to one side and take hold of her hand with my free one. Once we get outside she gives my hand a squeeze and lets go.

"I'm not going to say anything to Dad about that, and I don't want you to either," she says.

"About what?"

"Right," she says.

We're crossing the hot parking lot toward the car. After the banners and fountains and piped-in music of the mall, the asphalt and glare outside seem like part of an essential, biblical landscape. The stiff twine handles of the shopping bags cut into my fingers. The coffee and sugar have made me jumpy. My feet are hot, and I feel tired and cranky. I can sense my mother, that peculiar love of my life, starting to slip off one edge of the world, and the children I am not going to have, those cherubic monsters, slipping off the other.

"Almost there," my mother says as the car comes into view. "We're almost there."

# As Needed

<hr/>

I was sitting on a subway train out of Times
Square, fanning myself with a chewed-up copy of *The Great
Gatsby* and trying to remember if I had ever been this hot in my
life and when that might have been. The subway kept slamming
me in all directions and the effort to hold my balance made me
so angry I was almost crying. I stared down at the red-and-white
striped skirt my mother had made over for me that I had once
liked. It was limp and wrinkled and it made me look fat. I wanted
to go home and burn it but I could not afford to: I had only four
work skirts.

It was 1980, my first year out of college, and I was doing temp
work in a law office and writing for an obscure community weekly

that no one I knew read. It was not the life I had always imagined. At school my friends and I had longed for the real world, that magical place where we would find meaningful work and in time, we each privately assumed, become famous. At parties we'd stand around the keg on someone's back porch, so hot from dancing that we'd be steaming in the night air like horses, pawing and stamping, impatient for our future to get there. We'd pass cigarettes and joints back and forth and tell each other what it was going to be like.

On the train I opened the book and read the scene where Gatsby is throwing his expensive shirts all over the room. *"They're such beautiful shirts," she sobbed, her voice muffled in the thick folds.* I had once thought this was a lovely, tragic passage; now it struck me as melodramatic and silly. Across from me a woman was engrossed in a book I wished I were reading instead, something with a title that swirled passionately across its cover. She wore nurse's shoes and nylons as thick as tights and she frowned at the print as she read.

The doors squealed open at Seventy-second Street and people pushed each other in and out. A tall man in a dark suit grabbed the bar over my head. I felt the whisper of his pants against my legs. He was trying to manage a newspaper, a briefcase, and a bunch of flowers wrapped in green waxed paper. I met his eyes and saw his lips move.

"What?"

"I said can you beat it? Can you beat this heat?" he said. I thought, all things considered, he looked remarkably cool.

"You could take your jacket off."

"What?"

"Your jacket." I pantomimed. He nodded and winked, something that had not happened to me since I was about five.

He handed me his briefcase and slid gracefully out of his jacket. The leather of the case felt smooth and important on my lap. I ran my fingers over it.

"I'm Carl." In his shirtsleeves, his hand held out toward me, he looked good enough to run for office.

"Emily," I said, shaking his hand. Firmly, I thought.

"Emily," he said. "My mother's name."

I smiled, although I hate that sort of sweet talk.

I looked back at my book, opened now on top of the briefcase. It gave us a peculiar sort of intimacy.

"Great book, right?" he shouted down toward me.

I nodded.

"Never read it," he said. "Saw the movie. Great car."

"You should," I said. "It's a classic."

He nodded. "You even sound like my mother." He winked again and smiled broadly. His whole face seemed to brag about his teeth, which were as white as his shirt, the whitest teeth I had ever seen in my life. I remember thinking absurdly, I will miss those teeth.

The subway threw us all forward at Ninety-sixth Street and knocked us back. We shook our heads and smiled at each other, united in this tiny misery, and he headed toward the door.

I watched him thread his way through the crowd, the briefcase still on my lap.

The elevator in my building was broken. I started climbing the stairs and felt a wall of heat hit me on the fourth-floor landing, where a little girl in underpants was riding a tricycle like a scooter down the hallway, standing on the back step and pushing off with one bare foot against the tiled floor. Plastic tassels fluttered from the handlebar grips.

On my floor my neighbor Ruth had her door propped open as far as the chain would allow. Her cocker spaniel, Charlie, had wedged himself against the opening and I could hear him breathing like an asthmatic in the shadows. Ruth gave him pills for his heart twice a day and fried up hamburger for him at night. In the evening they sat together on the front steps of the apartment building, Ruth cooling them both with a big fan that had cherry trees painted on it.

Charlie whimpered slightly as I coaxed the key into the lock of my door. "It's okay," I said. "It's only me."

My apartment was small enough to memorize in a single glance, and after a year there was no longer anything romantic or courageous about living there. After a long shower, I turned the fan on high and sat on the bed with a beer, drinking for a while and staring at the briefcase.

When I finally nudged the latch, it flipped open with an expensive click, a sound that reminded me of TV movies about successful executives and their unhappy marriages. Inside were a stack of file folders, copies of *Forbes* and *Sports Illustrated*, several pens, a datebook, a pack of Camel filters, some breath spray, and an amber-colored prescription bottle. Carl's last name, Wright, was typed on the label, along with the drug's name, which I didn't recognize, and the phrase "as needed."

I pulled a cigarette from the pack and got his number from Information. His voice answered after three rings, instructing me to leave my name and number at the tone, assuring me that he was sorry to have missed my call.

I followed his instructions, then closed the leather case and set it on my desk, where it looked sophisticated and foreign next to the spiral notebooks and battered paperbacks.

In the kitchen I opened the tiny refrigerator and crouched in front of the faint blast of cool air. The lettuce and vegetables looked so difficult in their plastic bags that I settled for a cheese sandwich and ate in front of the television with the plate on my lap. Outside, twilight was falling with an eerie brightness that made me think of all the things that were going on in the city and how little I had done that whole long day. I had that confused feeling of wanting the phone to ring and yet not being able to think of anyone I really wanted to talk to.

I had another sandwich and another beer, and when it was finally dark I made myself turn on the light and go to my desk. It was littered with all the information and quotes I needed for an article I was doing for the community paper on rent stabilization and renters' rights. I knew it was an article few people would read; it mostly repeated what had been said a thousand times before. Jerry, the editor, told me we would flag it on the front page and run it with a photo, but with a readership as small as ours I knew this would make little difference. That sort of remark pained him. "Go ahead, Emily. Curse the darkness," he would say, crossing his arms over his chest protectively.

Tonight I sat at the desk with the pack of forbidden Camels and bribed myself through two pages. My head was already light with nicotine when the phone rang around eleven.

"Hello, this is Emily," I said in a flat voice. "I'm sorry I'm not available right now but I *would* like to return your call. Please leave your name and number when you hear the beep." I followed this with a little machinelike bleat.

I listened to Carl leave his message. He sounded like a talk-radio host—chatty, friendly, vaguely Midwestern, someone you could talk to about acid rain or violence in the schools. He sounded like someone who was faking sincerity and almost pulling it off. Almost.

I smoked my way through two more uninspired paragraphs and then turned the lamp off and sat in the dark watching Johnny Carson with the sound off. A pretty woman in a low-cut gown was singing, the sequins on her dress popping like flashbulbs in the lights. Watching her I thought of the hours I had spent in front of my bedroom mirror at home, holding a make-believe microphone in one hand and, to heighten the realism, periodically straightening out the make-believe cord with the other.

At the next set of commercials I called Carl.

"Here you are, a grown woman in New York City, and you don't know a briefcase from an attaché case?" was the first thing he said to me.

"I'm not the one who left whatever you want to call it on a total stranger's lap on the *subway*," I said.

"Hey, don't knock it. I've met a lot of attractive women this way." When I didn't say anything, he said, "I'm kidding, of course. I'm just joking." Another pause. "I'm from Nebraska."

So we talked for a while. He told me he had come to New York to make a fortune in investment banking.

"And is it working?" I said.

"Well, that's the amazing thing," he said, sounding amazed. "It is."

I told him the name of the paper I worked on, trying to make it sound like a paying job without actually lying. He had never heard of it. "But I get the picture," he said. "You're out to save the world from bastards like me."

"More from the system that *creates* bastards like you," I said.

"Thank you," he said. "That helps."

We agreed to meet for breakfast. He thanked me for calling, and then he said, "Good night, Emily."

The sound of my name reeled me in like a fish. He said it in just two syllables, as though he were already used to it, as though he had been saying it for years.

I put the briefcase—attaché case—on the kitchen counter next to the toaster before going to bed, so that the dark bulk of it would not keep me awake. I turned the fan off and noticed that it had grown surprisingly quiet in the street. A single siren, blocks away, rose and weakened to silence within a few seconds, leaving the night so quiet I thought I could hear Charlie whimpering in his sleep next door.

In bed, waiting for sleep, I saw Carl swaying for balance above me, one hand wrapped around the pole and the other clutching a funnel of green waxed paper. I found myself wondering where he had been tonight and who the flowers had been for. Whom.

---

I bumped through the revolving door with the attaché case and saw him sitting at a booth in the back, his suit jacket hanging on a hook behind him, his newspaper propped up against the sugar dispenser. He looked like an ad for himself, down to the pinpoint of light glinting off his collar bar. In the leftover early-morning heat, he was the only person in the diner who did not look damp and cranky.

I walked toward him behind a waitress who stopped at his table with a plate of food and a coffeepot. He said something I couldn't hear and she smiled.

"Emily," he announced when he saw me, bobbing up as much as the booth would allow.

"Don't get up," I said.

"You smell nice."

"It's soap," I lied.

"Something else here?" the waitress asked. I ordered coffee and she filled my cup and walked away.

"You ought to eat something. Breakfast is an incredibly important meal," Carl said. "Don't tell me you're dieting. Women are always dieting."

I was trying to lose five pounds but I would never have said so. "I'm not hungry. Thank you."

"You look fine. You look great." He waved his fork at me.

"Women like you shouldn't be too thin. Here, eat this." He pushed a plate of buttered toast toward me. "Really. I can't eat all this."

"Cufflinks?" I stared at his extended arm. I had never been out with a man who wore cufflinks.

Carl reached across the table and patted my hand. "If you're good, I'll show you my tie tack later."

"Well, here it is." I patted the attaché case on the seat next to me. It was beginning to feel like mine, like an expensive leather lap dog.

"Great. Super. Thanks," he said. "Look, can't I buy you *something*? An English muffin at least?"

I shook my head. "I'm late for work as it is." I wanted him to know that my life was not unimportant.

He nodded sympathetically. "I guess even exposing injustice and championing the people can get to be a grind after a while." He grinned and I got another look at those fabulous teeth.

"I love my work," I said, forgetting for a moment my many dissatisfactions with the paper and the fact that the work I was late for was the full-time temp job that I hated. "At least I believe in something besides my salary."

I stared at the toast, gone soft in the middle where the butter had melted. I felt a flash of hunger. When I looked up, Carl was still smiling.

"I love earnest women," he said.

"I'll bet."

Mutual mistrust is not a bond, I kept trying to remind myself.

When I got up to leave he said he would call me and I said, "Why?"

He pointed his finger at me. "I like you, Em. I really do."

I laid a hand on his shoulder and felt the smooth, tight weave of his shirt. "I know better than to believe that," I said. "Thank God."

---

After work I dropped the story on renters' rights off at the paper. Jerry seemed to like it. "Great. Great," he said, glancing at it. "You really move in for the kill." He looked up from a desk ringed with empty styrofoam cups.

The story was nowhere near great but he loved the paper enough to wish that it was. I stuck around for a while out of respect for that, and because when you do not really believe, you have to work that much harder to prove that you do.

I decided to walk home to try to get back a sense of where I was, passing through neighborhoods instead of underneath them. By the time I got to my building it was dark. Charlie began to whine when he sensed me on the other side of the door, and I could hear Ruth sweep across the room in her bedroom slippers. She was a big woman and her feet barely left the ground when she moved.

"How's the boy?" I asked.

Ruth shook her head and spoke softly, as though she didn't want him to hear. "Cholley's having a bad night. It's this heat. And that g.d. elevator's on the fritz again. We take turns carrying each other on the stairs." She prodded the dog lightly with the toe of her flowered slipper. "Isn't that right, old boy?"

"How about coming next door to watch TV later? The change of scene might do him good."

Ruth looked suspicious for a moment. She plugged her fists into the pockets of her housecoat. "Johnny Carson?"

I nodded. "Whatever."

She looked at Charlie. "We'll be over later," she said.

Ruth brought two Dr. Peppers over and the three of us settled on the bed, Charlie curled against his mistress. He had a reassuring dog smell about him. We watched Johnny Carson, and when Ruth giggled, Charlie's head bobbed in her lap.

———

That Saturday Ruth and I rode to the vet in a cab, Charlie breathing noisily between us. The vet was a sad-looking man with long sideburns. He lifted the dog onto the stainless-steel examining table and listened to him breathe. "It's time, Ruth," he said, and Ruth nodded and held the dog close.

"I wish I could explain it to him," she said, crying. "I wish I could make him understand."

Ruth held her dog and told him all the things she needed to hear herself say while the vet worked quietly beside her. A dog barked somewhere in the building and Charlie passed from what was left of life to death, Ruth's warm breath against his ear.

On our way home, she stared out the window of the cab. Her black tee shirt and black stretch pants were covered with the dog's blond fur.

"We should never have come," she said, her head still turned away. I could hardly hear her over the traffic sliding around us. "He would still be alive."

"Oh, Ruth," I said. "You did the right thing. He wasn't going to get better. He was in pain and you helped him."

She turned to look at me. "How do you know?" she said. "It's fine for you to talk about right and wrong. You don't know. You have no idea." She snatched at the fur on her pants. Each time she shook her fingers free of a clump of it, it flew back to her clothes. "I *loved* that dog," she said finally, shutting me out.

I knew I had somehow said the wrong thing, and I felt angry and sad. We each held fast to our own door handles for balance, between us the empty stretch of seat where the dog had lain on the ride over.

---

Ruth didn't want company so I went home and sat at my desk rearranging the stacks of papers and notes, organizing the books according to height. The phone rang. It was Carl, asking me if I wanted to go to dinner.

"What's the matter? Did your real date stand you up?"

"Emily, has anyone ever told you what an unusual phone manner you have?"

We agreed to meet at a dressed-up diner in his neighborhood, a place where the booths were equipped with white tablecloths and jukeboxes. I got there early, hoping for the first ten minutes that he wouldn't come and then, for the next ten, fearing it.

He did come, looking like God's idea of civilized man. Just because we're fallen doesn't mean we can't dress well, I thought. He carried a fistful of daisies wrapped in green paper.

"You sounded on the phone like you needed these."

"You shouldn't have done that," I said. I did not feel strong enough to handle that sort of kindness from a man I didn't trust.

We drank wine and talked politics and religion; he called me naive and I called him reactionary.

"I can't believe I'm having dinner with a man who actually voted for Richard Nixon," I said.

"You're having dinner with a man who volunteered for duty in Vietnam."

I did not believe this.

"Want to see my scars?" he said.

"No," I said. "Jesus. No, I do not want to see your scars." I felt that he was somehow turning things to his advantage and it made me feel mean. "What are those pills for, the ones in your *attaché* case?"

"Those," he said, and when he stopped to take a breath I knew we were headed under the surface of something. "Those are what I take when I feel like killing myself. Do you ever have days like that?"

I swallowed and waited to hear my own answer. "No," I said. "But sometimes I think I'm starting."

Neither of us said anything after that, and then he reached in his pocket and handed me a quarter. I picked some Patsy Cline and Nat King Cole, and, blessedly, our food arrived. Carl ate like a high-school kid, swallowing his food in big, unconscious bites and wiping his mouth wholesale with a pink napkin from time to time. He didn't seem as much like the enemy, eating. I liked watching him.

We split the check and Carl guided me out of the restaurant with his hand at the small of my back. I had not felt the pressure of a hand there in a long time, and something in me went weak. Outside, it was cooler than it had been in days, and a breeze seemed to be blowing the dead air out. Carl put his arm around me. I leaned into him with a feeling of honest relief, as though I had been running a relay for miles and had finally tagged my partner. For that moment the outcome of the race was unimportant; I was happy simply not to be running.

We made a slow zigzag of the long and short Manhattan blocks and finally Carl stopped in front of an apartment building and said, "This is where I live." A young couple sat on the broad cement steps, smoking. The boy's voice carried in a gentle hum and the girl laughed softly.

Carl turned to face me. "I want you to come up," he said, "but I'm not going to talk you into it."

I wanted something else to pass between us before I went upstairs, some promise or confession, but he moved on ahead of me and stood quietly, holding the glass door open against his back, waiting.

"Come on, Emily," he said finally. He held out his hand.

I took it.

---

Upstairs he did not bother to show me the apartment or offer me something to drink. We walked through darkened rooms to the bedroom, where he sat me down on the edge of the bed.

We sat breathing for a bit with the awkwardness of it, and then I began to unbutton his shirt. It felt supple and exceptionally smooth in the dark, and in my fear and desire it seemed like the most beautiful material I had ever touched. Underneath, the skin of his chest was marked with ridges like the lines of a map, scars. I traced them with my fingers and tried not to think.

We made something akin to love and once he was asleep I edged myself beyond the reach of his long limbs and crept quietly out of bed. In the next room I turned on a lamp. The attaché case lay centered on the blotter of a huge wooden desk. In the corner were two photographs in heavy silver frames, one of a family gathered around a picnic table, the other of a smiling young woman sitting on a couch, her legs tucked up next to her.

I turned out the light and went back to bed, quieting myself to the sound of Carl's even breathing. I could not tell if the lack I felt was for something that had been lost, or taken from me, or given away. I lay there and thought about going home, and then I realized I had no idea where I was or how, exactly, I had gotten there. It would have to wait until morning. The ceiling disappeared into darkness and I stared up toward it and thought, dear God, please don't let me die here in this bed, in this apartment.

# *All These Gifts*

---

When the news that Dinah was getting involved with a married man fired through the family, her brother, Cal, called to remind her that men were like buses: there would be another one along in five minutes. He was handsome and affable, and he was speaking from personal experience.

"Cal doesn't know what he's talking about," Dinah's sister, Park, said later. She had just turned thirty-five, and had had her hair frosted. "You've got to grab at all you can in this life. The wife isn't your responsibility."

Dinah's mother was tickled to be let in on the secret. "There are no accidents, honey. You invited this into your life. So did he.

And so did she." She hugged her daughter and said over her shoulder, "It'll be a hard lesson, but it'll be worth it."

No one told her father, who could not be expected to understand. He got all news of the family through his wife, who broke it into manageable bites, as though she were cutting up a lamb chop for a child. His wife was not fazed by his success in the corporate world beyond their driveway, by the high price that was put on his legal counsel. She referred to the company he kept in boardrooms as "the crowd your father runs around with," and maintained that it kept him insulated from the real world, by which she meant plumbers who would charge you seventy dollars an hour to pull artichoke leaves out of your disposal or old women who needed rides to the grocery store every week.

"There's no sense burdening your father with what we can't make him understand," she said. She hugged Dinah again and offered to make her a sandwich.

"He means a lot to me, Mom," Dinah said, leaning on the counter while her mother rooted through the refrigerator. "I wouldn't do something like this otherwise."

"We all have to do what we all have to do," her mother said.

It irked Dinah that her mother did not seem more bothered. "But this is wrong, isn't it?" she said. "An affair with a married man?"

"Of course it's wrong. Is this the first mistake you've ever made? The first bad thing that makes it hard to get to sleep, that shakes you awake in the middle of the night?" Sandra Fortune waved a knife at her daughter on the other side of the butcher-block island. "Dinah, honey, this is life. You learn to live with guilt. You do the best you can. Believe me, you don't get away with anything in this life. You're going to pay the price, so you make sure you get your money's worth."

Dinah dutifully ate her sandwich, wondering when this particular ritual would turn itself around, when she might begin making sandwiches for her mother in some cheery kitchen beyond the reach of her imagination of the future. It frightened her to think of pouring her mother a glass of buttermilk and helping her in and out of the car. She would buy her colorful brooches in department stores, butterflies and birds that sparkled with chips of glass. That was part of paying the price for the sandwich she was eating now, for the underwear and sweaters her mother bought her and left on the bed in the room her parents kept for her in her absence, in case she ever wanted or needed to "come home." In return she owed her parents visits and phone calls; eventually, when they moved to a smaller house, her brother would put up shelves for them and she would bring her father twenty-five-pound sacks of birdseed; she would buy him bird books and binoculars that he would appreciate and never use.

"How do you know Dad wouldn't understand?" Dinah asked, looking out the window to where her father was dragging a hose across the grass toward his vegetable garden.

Her mother was sweeping the countertop with a damp dishrag and she turned to face Dinah, a collection of crumbs held in her cupped hand. "He's a decent and fair man, and probably the most generous person I've ever known," her mother began. This was the preamble she always used to introduce any criticism of her husband, a litany of qualities that seemed somehow part of the faults that followed. "But he loves principle more than people. He loves loyalty and devotion and integrity. You know Dad, you know that about him. He would want your respect for the marriage to outweigh your affection for the man. People don't sleep around in your father's moral universe."

"I'm not sleeping *around*."

"I know that. I'm trying to explain how your father would see it. It would disappoint him to tears. He thinks the world of you, you know."

Just as word of their children's failures and successes had always flowed through Sandra en route to her husband, the spoken measure of his love had similarly traveled through her to them. At Christmas he always smiled with exaggerated cheerfulness at the gifts from his children. "Well," he would say, nodding and turning toward his wife. "That's very thoughtful." And he would set the box aside and gently toss the balled-up wrapping paper into the fire. He was, above all else, a gentle man. Later, Sandra would telephone the three children in turn, telling them how much Dad had enjoyed the robe or garden tools or bentwood rocker, how he could not stop talking about it. Each year, Dinah and Cal and Park would spend more money than they had the last, hoping perhaps to beat him at his own game. One year it was a stereo, then a television set, then a selection of expensive French wines. These gestures were always dwarfed in turn by the piles of gifts that appeared every year under the tree from their father, and the "happy cabbage" he slipped into envelopes. Each year they were more than reimbursed for their generosity, and by late afternoon, when the ceremony was complete, they kicked sheepishly through the debris of shiny paper and curled ribbon on the living-room rug to kiss and hug one another and sit down to Christmas dinner.

"This has gotten out of hand," Sandra would say to Dinah later. "It's obscene, all these gifts, all that money."

It was a sincere if desperate gesture, but it was ultimately unsatisfying, and the disappointment began to weigh heavily as the three grown children loaded their bounty into their cars to drive home, everyone feeling somehow sad and guilty and full of love they still could not express. "Merry Christmas," they wished each other, and "Drive safely," and then they each took off into the night, and Dinah imagined that her parents drifted slowly back into the house where they split a beer and sat quietly for a few minutes watching the tree lights blink.

———— ————

Dinah and her mother spent whole afternoons together when Dinah was home visiting, sitting in the sewing room and paging through pattern books, their iced-tea glasses leaving water circles on the cutting table. Sandra would unwind bolts of fabric and finger it with a delicacy she brought to no other task. "It feels like silk," she said. "But it's polyester. You can throw it in the washing machine."

Sandra had no respect for sheer beauty. She couldn't touch silk without thinking of dry cleaning or enjoy the gleam of silver without anticipating the inevitable tarnish and polishing. Visiting the Vanderbilt mansion with Dinah one summer, she had leaned over and whispered, "Just think of the work keeping a place like this up."

Sandra stood in front of the mirror now, the fabric draped over her shoulder like a toga. It was a deep, rich blue with flecks of silver-gray that matched her hair.

"It's lovely," Dinah said. "I wish it really was silk."

"No one will know it's not."

"You will."

"You remind me of Lee," Sandra said. Lee was a friend of Sandra's from years ago, when the kids were little and Sandra and Jack would go for weeks without so much as going out for dinner or a movie. "I'd be walking down the street with Park pushing Cal in the stroller, you on my hip, looking an absolute fright, the permanent completely out of my hair so I had to wear a bandanna on my head like some sort of Depression farm woman. And there'd be Lee, washing the windows in her cashmere sweater. 'Lee,' I'd say. 'You'll ruin that sweater.' And she'd say in that slow voice of hers, 'Sandra, honey, I'm not washing the windows with my sweater.' What a character. Poor Lee."

"What happened to her again?"

"Well, her first husband committed suicide, you know. And then Walt died of a heart attack on that cruise. On their honeymoon."

"That's awful," Dinah said. Her mother seemed to have a million of these stories.

"Oh, it was. It was. And she had a heart of gold. She loved you kids. She used to come over and braid your hair and tie it up in ribbons. You don't remember that?"

"Vaguely." Dinah had no recollection of it, but it seemed unkind to say so.

"She about saved my life. She'd take you kids for an hour when I was at my wits' end, just so I could go downtown. Dad wouldn't let me have a sitter and I had you kids on my hands day in and day out."

There was an awkward silence as the conversation threatened to turn down familiar roads, rutted over the years with the accusations and frustrations of hindsight. Dinah finally stood and picked up her sweaty glass, jiggling it to free the ice cubes.

"I wish I had those days to do over again," Sandra said, looking out the window at nothing in particular. "I'd do it differently. I wouldn't let myself get so tired."

"You can't say that now, Mom. Everybody did their best." Dinah was trying to preserve a past she couldn't remember and couldn't afford to feel guilty about now, when her conscience was already overbooked with more immediate appointments. "The dress is going to be beautiful," she said gently.

"Yes, it is." Sandra's voice had an odd determination in it, but Dinah noticed that her hands, as they wound the material back on the bolt, were spotted and lined. "This polyester will do just fine."

---

At least once during the summer, the whole family got together at Sandra and Jack's house for dinner. This event was usually loosely yoked to some holiday to lend it greater credibility as an official family gathering, and to give it a sense of purpose. It provided a reason for drinking champagne and eating in the dining room and prompted a certain dedication to the spirit of celebration.

This year they were reuniting in honor of Independence Day, and Dinah was giving Cal a ride because his car could not be trusted on the freeway. She wore a dress her mother had made for her, and nylons, even though it had to be close to ninety outside. She compensated for the conservative cut of the dress— what her mother referred to as "classic" lines that would never go out of style—with bright plastic earrings that had been made from fishing lures. It was the sort of small compromise that cordial family dinners depended on.

She stood waiting for her brother in his living room, her stockings fused to her legs with heat and perspiration. "God, it's hot in here. How do you stand it?"

Cal tore around his apartment, oblivious, searching for his keys and wallet. The living room was littered with clothes, musical equipment, photographs, bank statements, foil-wrapped throat lozenges. He plucked a plastic bottle of vitamins from the disarray on the kitchen table and tossed it at Dinah. "Here, take a few of these. There's something going around."

"Whatever it is, it's probably breeding in here." Dinah shook out two vitamins.

"Yuk, yuk." Cal disappeared into the bedroom. "I had a fire in here last week, did I tell you?"

Dinah thought the apartment did look like the sort of place that would be featured in a filmstrip to be shown during National Fire Prevention Week. "No. What happened?"

"Typical stovetop blaze. But I was in the music room practicing, with the headphones on and the door closed. I could've lost everything. The television saved my life. I had it on with the sound turned down. Suddenly this big fire comes on the screen and I started to *smell* smoke." Cal stuck his blond head out the bedroom doorway, an unknotted tie swinging loosely from his neck. "Weird." He disappeared again and Dinah heard the grating sound of a closet door being pulled shut off its track.

"Cal, let's go. We'll be late."

He darted from the bedroom across the hall to the bathroom and reemerged with a toothbrush sticking out of his mouth. "It's cool. They expect me to be late. It's one of the few expectations they have of me that I can actually meet." He ducked back into the bathroom.

"That's not true." Dinah was beginning to feel dizzy in the heat of the stuffy, cluttered room.

Cal came down the short hall and veered into the kitchen, his untied shoelaces ticking against the linoleum. "I know, I know. Dad thinks the world of you kids." He duplicated their mother's cadence without the exaggeration of mockery.

Dinah heard the refrigerator door swing open. "Cal, come *on*."

"We're going. Do you want one of these?" His long tanned arm shot from the kitchen doorway. At the end of it, in the sinewy cushion of his hand, was a small bottle of exotic fruit juice.

"No thanks, maybe just a sip of yours. We've got to get going."

"I'll bring two. Okay, okay."

The phone rang. "Don't get that," Cal said, striding toward the door. "It'll be them. We'll say we ran into traffic, we passed an accident."

"After you," he said, holding the door open. "You look nice."

---

"They're getting older," Dinah said. She was driving, her body tensed and alert as it always was when she had other people in her car, other lives she was responsible for.

"Who isn't, babe." Cal squinted at the traffic around them. "Who. Isn't."

"Not just older. They're getting *old*. Do you ever listen to Mom talk about their friends? Everybody they know is either dead or dying or has Alzheimer's. She knows more widows than she does wives."

"Dad isn't even seventy yet."

"He drinks, he doesn't exercise, he eats practically nothing but red meat—"

"But look at him. He looks great. He's got the right karma going for him. He's lucky all the way down to his name."

"He's just a man, Cal. He's going to die someday."

"And so are we. We could die today. In this car, on this freeway. On our way home to visit our aging parents. And they might die on the way back from our funeral."

"Stop it."

Cal had his arm out the window, gliding forward and back in a gesture of arm wrestling with the wind. "Look, all I'm saying is you can't think about that stuff. You live clean, you do your work, you go to dinner when your parents invite you. Someday you'll have kids and you'll give back what you can." He turned to face her profile. "Are you still seeing that guy?"

Dinah didn't answer.

"Dinah. Dinah. Dinah."

Dinah shot into the fast lane and felt her foot sink powerfully into the accelerator. The pack of cars they had been traveling with suddenly fell away.

"Don't lecture me," she said. "I know it's wrong."

"I don't care about that, Dinah. I'm just worried that you're tying up the phone lines with a man you can't have. Maybe somebody else is trying to get through."

They rode quietly for a while. The hot air whistled deafeningly through the car and Dinah realized that her throat was sore from shouting to be heard. When they finally got off the freeway, she felt her neck and shoulders relax. "Don't you ever worry that Dad's going to die before you get a chance to prove something to him?"

"Is that what this is all about? I made my peace with all that. I had to. As far as Dad's concerned, the evolution of music topped out with Glenn Miller. I could have a top-ten song on every AM station in the country and Dad would never even know it. The man couldn't name a rock band if he was in a jail cell and his life depended on it. He couldn't even tell you who was in the Beatles."

"Oh, come on." Dinah turned toward her brother while they waited for the light to change. He was chomping furiously on a stick of gum.

"He couldn't. I asked him once."

"You *asked* him?" Dinah blushed, realizing she had never asked her father a question she thought he might not be able to answer.

"The point is, why should he know? Can you name the top five law firms in the U.S.? Can you name even one? We live in different worlds, Dinah. The man never leaves the house without a briefcase. What's he going to do, cruise into a record store and flip through the CDs? What would he do with his briefcase, check it at the counter with the backpacks?" Cal beat out a quick rhythm on the dashboard with his fingertips. "To hell with that."

Dinah thought of the long hours her brother spent practicing, surrounded by the massive black boxes of his trade. He had no car to speak of, and he had a saucepan sitting in his bathroom sink because the drain didn't work, but he kept himself outfitted with the finest keyboards money could buy. "Groups don't want to know how well you can play," he had told her once. "They want to know what you've got." He played with two bands; if he wasn't at a gig he was practicing at home; if he wasn't learning a song, he was writing one; if he wasn't playing music, he was listening to it. It was all he did and all he seemed to care about.

Dinah turned the car into her parents' driveway, bordered by an ivy-covered fence on one side and several brilliant bursts of azaleas on the other. Cal was staring straight ahead, absentmindedly feeding another stick of gum into his mouth. And here's a man who's made his peace with all that, Dinah thought, watching him. Heaven help the well adjusted.

---

Jack Fortune's hand shook as he poured champagne over the slices of homegrown peaches in each glass. Dinah glanced toward Cal, trying to get his attention, but his focus was fixed on the television, where a man in a cardigan hunched over a putter and rocked back and forth from foot to foot.

Park and Sandra came in from the kitchen, both wiping their hands on their aprons. "Is anyone watching this?" Park asked, punching the knob on the television. Her movements were punctuated by the clatter of a series of wooden bracelets she wore on her arm. She bought all her jewelry in foreign countries, favoring jade and tiger's eye and solid gold; she traveled frequently and had a lot of jewelry to show for it, and she was careful to bring back presents for everyone from each new country she visited. She had a good job in public relations; she had never been married, and she had invested wisely. "Thank God," Jack had said when she announced her latest promotion. "A child who can provide for us in our old age." Dinah knew he was really thanking God that he had at least one child whom he wouldn't have to continue providing *for* in old age.

They all raised their glasses. After the first ceremonial sip, Park and Sandra returned to the kitchen to "check on things," and Cal and Jack turned the golf match back on, although it was a sport neither followed or cared about much. Dinah trailed after her mother and sister to the kitchen, where she perched herself on a counter and drank her champagne.

"These peaches are great," she said, fishing out the slices with her fingers.

"Dad says after the cost of pruning and mulching and paying a gardener once a week, then losing half of them to the birds and squirrels, they only cost us about fifteen dollars apiece." Sandra rubbed a garlic clove in circles in the salad bowl.

"Is every pleasure around here measured in terms of cost?" Dinah asked.

"Only the expensive ones," Park said, refilling their glasses from the dark-green bottle. "Of course, he makes up for it with this godawful champagne."

Sandra pulled the lid off a plastic container of marinated green beans and sniffed at them. "Park, taste one of these," she said, stabbing the beans with a fork. "See if they taste funny to you."

Sandra held the fork out toward Park, who nibbled at the end of it like a fish. "They're awfully bitter," she said.

Sandra nodded and then began shaking her head, then nodded

again. She carried the beans to the sink and spooned them down the garbage disposal. "They're from your father's damn garden. He keeps picking them and I keep throwing them out and replacing them with beans from the grocery store."

"Why don't you just tell him they're not good?" Dinah asked. She was examining the bloated reflection of her face in the toaster.

"You know your father," Sandra said. "I tried. He says they're fine. He says that's the way homegrown green beans are supposed to taste."

"He's out of his mind," Park said. Her wooden bracelets knocked cleanly against each other as she buttered a long loaf of French bread.

"It doesn't seem fair to deceive him that way," Dinah said. She imagined her parents sitting down to dinner, her father's pride and delight over the steaming green beans and her mother's artful enthusiasm.

"For God's sake, Dinah," Sandra said, "I'm just trying to keep the peace and get by. Don't make me feel like such a criminal."

"For crying out loud," Park echoed. "Since when are you the arbiter of honesty and decency?" Park and her mother exchanged a brief look, and Dinah guessed that her affair with the married man had been a subject of much discussion between them. Suddenly she was the kind of woman who. Suddenly the world was divided into two kinds of people—those who honored the sanctity of marriage and those who didn't.

---

Dinner was given over to political issues, family reminiscences, and praise for the garden vegetables. Sandra and Jack sat at opposite ends of the table, sharing that unnameable resemblance that comes to people who have spent close to forty years together. When Jack spoke, he spoke to Sandra alone; her glances and nods answered his. He seemed unaware of his children who flanked him, who leaned toward him when he talked, their eyebrows lifted in anticipation, their knives and forks arrested in midair.

No one complained at these dinners and no one argued. No secrets were revealed and Sandra kept the pauses from growing into silences. Jack told Sandra about a strange pro bono case the firm was handling; Sandra asked Cal about his bands, whether they had any gigs lined up; Cal answered in a few words and asked his father what he thought of the Giants' rookie centerfielder. There was a brief round of recollected elementary-school teachers, family pets, and former neighbors—the inevitable conflict of memories.

Cal and Dinah began clearing the table as their parents and Park shared the last of the wine.

"Did you see the way his hand shakes?" Dinah said, filing plates in the dishwasher. "Did you see?"

Cal was bent over the sink scrubbing a pot, his tie thrown over his shoulder to keep it out of the soapy water. "It's the drugs he takes for his blood pressure. Give it a rest, Dinah. Dad's fine."

"You're worried, too. You just won't admit it."

"Look. Here's a man who's been relatively happily married to the same woman all his adult life. He has three reasonably intelligent, reasonably loyal kids who've never been in trouble with the law. He makes more money in a day than I see in a month. And he has the respect of his peers. Meanwhile, I'm on the wrong side of thirty in a business that expects people to die before they grow up, I'm living like a college kid, I don't have a wife. I don't even have health insurance. And I should be worried about *him*?"

His hands darted about the sink as he spoke, the water rising in waves over the lip of the dishpan to splash against his clothes. By the time he finished speaking, his shirtfront was drenched. "Christ," he said, looking down. They both began to laugh.

―――――――

Cal had brought a new pair of pants with him that needed to be shortened, and after dinner he retreated to the sewing room with Sandra and Park. From the kitchen, where she was finding room in the crowded refrigerator for the last of the leftovers, Dinah saw her father slip out the back door toward the garden, an ancient transistor radio in his hand.

When she joined him a few minutes later, he was examining the apples scattered across the wide circle of ground under the tree. Many of the fruits were nearly whole, abandoned by animals that had taken one small bite and changed their minds. The radio was neatly balanced in the crotch of the tree, tuned to a base-ball game.

"Dad?" Dinah said.

It seemed to take him a moment to recognize her. "Well, this is a surprise," he said, as though she had just arrived and they had not been sitting at the same dinner table twenty minutes earlier. He wiped his forehead with a handkerchief and turned back toward his garden. "Can you use a few tomatoes?"

The plant shook as he twisted a tomato free; he placed it in her hand. "Look at that. You won't find them like that in any grocery store."

The fruit was heavy and still warm in her palm, and the skin strained to contain it. Her father returned with two more and a handful of cherry tomatoes, so ripe they had begun to split.

She went to place them on the grass nearby and when she turned back to her father, he was bent over the cucumber plant like a quarterback in the huddle, rustling through the flat prickly leaves. "Here's a nice one," he said, rubbing his hand over the stubble as he handed it to her. "Do you like eggplant?"

"You bet," Dinah said, although she had been allergic to it all her life. The radio sportscaster's voice grew excited and the crowd cheered from its perch in the tree; Jack Fortune seemed not to notice as his hands moved among the glossy purple bulbs hanging like ornaments from the fragile plant. "Here," he called, and tossed it to her.

"Dad," she said, "go deep." She took a few paces back, careful not to step on anything that looked intentionally planted. She lobbed the eggplant carefully; her father caught it with one hand and threw it back in the same motion. She added it to the small pile of other vegetables on the grass.

Her father pulled a handkerchief from his pocket and mopped the back of his neck. His bifocals dropped to the end of his nose.

"Dad," Dinah said suddenly, "you know that guy I've been seeing? He's married."

A commercial for house paint filled the air. Her father tugged at a weed. "I know. Your mother told me." His hand grazed along the ground. "Next year we should just plant weeds," he said. "That would save us a lot of trouble, wouldn't it?"

Dinah dug her toes into her shoes and felt the sweat break out along her lip and eyebrows, at the small of her back. She began picking up the vegetables.

"You know, Dinah," her father said. She had her back to him. His voice sounded like it belonged to a much older man; it shook like his hands. "My father hated lawyers. He didn't understand the American legal system. He thought lawyers were greedy middlemen who stole from the honest and gave to the crooked. He belonged to a lodge and he paid in three dollars a month for almost fifty years, when three dollars was a fair sum of money for someone who worked on the highway. That was his insurance, he said, in case anything ever happened. When he finally got sick and they put him in the hospital, and I filed the forms for him to collect, do you know how much they were willing to pay? Fifty cents a day. Your mother and I were saving to buy our first home. We never went out, we never went to a movie or, God forbid, the theater. If we were really treating ourselves on the weekend we'd buy two paperback murder mysteries from the used-book store. We'd each read one and then we'd trade. That was a big weekend. And then my father landed in the hospital and there went our savings. And he had no idea, he just assumed the insurance was covering it."

Dinah sat on the grass and waited. The tomatoes were sending up their tart, garden smell.

"I went to visit him one day and—I never told this to another living soul—he was going on and on about how smart he had been to sign on with the lodge and how hospital life wasn't so bad as long as somebody else was paying for it. His voice was thin and he was too weak to laugh even. He was dying and no one would tell him; that was in the days when the patient was the last one to know. Finally he said he guessed it didn't take a hotshot lawyer to smell a good deal when one came along and I just started yelling at him. 'I'm paying for it,' I kept saying. 'I'm paying and Sandra's paying and the kids are paying.' He loved Sandra and he loved you kids and he started to cry. It was the only moment in my life I ever really wanted to take back. I stood there shaking and I thought that must be the worst moment that had ever happened on this earth.

"And now I look around at how things turned out, at everything I have. And I think, someday I'm going to die. I lie awake and think, someday I'll be walking down that dark hallway and my father will be at the other end. And I pray to God he won't be ashamed to see me."

Dinah stood up, the collection of fragrant vegetables precariously balanced in her arms. She and her father stood several feet apart, the tinny organ music from the seventh-inning stretch flowing through the space between them. At that moment, Jack Fortune, twenty years in the past and twenty years in the future, looked away into a corner of the yard, and his daughter, rooted in the present, knew no gift would ever bring them closer.

# My
# Real
# Life

Who knows how these things start? Last night we stayed too late and drank too much at a party, and today, a blindingly bright spring Saturday, we—my husband and I—are meandering around the local nursery, crunching up and down the gravel paths. My mouth feels painfully dried out, as if I've been sucking on paper towels, and I move along with the lightheaded, tentative energy of someone who is just beginning to recover from a long illness, stopping every few steps to take in the moist greenhouse air and gently finger the hardier plants.

Rob and I are in our thirties, and most of the parties we find ourselves at these years are dinner parties—cloth-napkin affairs set to a soundtrack of accessible jazz, decaffeinated coffee in the living room after dinner, all the guests back in their own homes by midnight. But last night we went to one of those parties that I hadn't been to since college, the sort where anyone who hears about it can consider himself invited, where you park the car a quarter-mile down the block and hear laughter and bass notes long before you reach the house, where people who didn't arrive together may leave together, where you go into a bedroom to get your coat and find a woman in a short black skirt searching the bedside drawers for a condom. At the parties Rob and I usually go to, people talk a lot about condoms but nobody ever actually brandishes one.

When we first got to this party, we stood around the kitchen for a while, drinking beer and casting about for someone we knew. Rob spotted a couple vaguely near our age and the four of us clustered near the sink and talked for an awkwardly long time about skiing. "Well," said the man finally, wagging his beer bottle by the neck, "I don't know about you, but I could use another one of these puppies." And the two of them eagerly escaped. Shortly after, a softball buddy of Rob's challenged him to a game of pool, and after they clambered down the basement stairs, I spent several minutes feigning interest in the notes and cartoons affixed to the refrigerator. I'm not sure what I was expecting to happen, but when I was sure it had failed to, I wandered into the living room to listen to music and count the number of people there who were as old as I was.

I had only been standing against the wall of the darkened room a couple minutes when a young man, who I figured was either stoned or being polite, asked me to dance. He had that lean look you see on the posters displayed in record stores, but he also looked like a boy who was capable of blushing; and one of his front teeth, I saw when he smiled, was tucked behind another in a way I found disarmingly fetching.

The song, which I had never heard before, was filled with disorienting pauses and German lyrics, giving it the quality of an overseas phone call with a poor connection. The beat eluded me, but the song was such a big favorite with the crowd that the boy and I were soon hemmed in, not so much dancing as upper-body swaying, like redwoods in a storm. We were pushed up against one another, practically touching, and I could feel the heat of him through his shirt. He's not stoned, I thought. And he's not being polite.

When the song ended, we danced to the next one, and after that, warm and out of breath, we went out the back door where a short flight of stairs led to the yard. I sat down with my arms around my legs, my chin on my knees. The boy stretched out next to me, his elbows resting behind him on the top step. He was tall: lying down, he covered the stairs.

I asked him about school, his family, his major. He wanted to know whether I believed in God, who I thought the greatest artists of all time were, if I had one day left to live how I would spend it. I answered his questions seriously. When he lifted his arm to point out the silhouette of a tree against the night sky, I felt the weightless, unintentional brush of his shirtsleeve against my folded leg. The nearness of him made me want to reach out and touch his hair.

We sat there a while longer. "I should go in," I finally said, standing up.

I didn't catch what he said, but I knew it was a question by the way his voice rose up at the end of it. He was still stretched out on the stairs, looking out toward the dark yard. Then his hand moved to touch my foot, shy yet secret, two fingers resting on the toe of my shoe.

For a few seconds I just stood there, feeling it. Then I said, "I better not," and I slid my foot out from under his hand and stepped quickly back to the noisy house. In my head was the lilt of the unheard question and the answer I had wanted to give, which was yes.

I found Rob in the kitchen, sitting at the table with my friend Joann. Joann is a slender woman and the effect of her clothes, which are all a little big, is unexpectedly sexy; her shirts and sweaters, with their rolled-up sleeves and deep V necks, all look borrowed or inherited from men. Tonight she had on a cashmere sweater with a tiny tear near the neck, and shoulder seams that ran several inches down her arms before her sleeves began. She was leaning toward Rob, across an array of beer bottles and a half-empty bowl of chips, her sleeves like wings resting at her sides. Rob was nodding and absentmindedly combing his hand across the place in back where his hair is thinning.

When Joann saw me she smiled and waved me over, and I sat

down between the two of them, my heart still pounding with guilt and desire. I steadied myself by watching them talk, my husband and my friend. I listened to the sound of my own pulse in my ears, and I took a drink every time one was offered.

---

In the nursery, a young woman with a scrubbed face and hair that could only be described as flaxen approaches and asks us if we need help. Both her hands are plugged shyly into the small front pocket of her green apron, but the pencil tucked behind her ear gives her a certain authority. Rob explains that we're here to look at "landscaping options," and when she begins to offer her opinion, I can tell he's all ears; right then I know we're going to end up with a backyard full of whatever this woman is selling. This annoys me since fixing up the yard was my idea in the first place, but I don't say anything; part of me is waiting for Rob to turn to me and ask me what I think, and part of me is expecting him not to. I must be looking for a fight, because I find myself hoping for the latter. In fact I retreat behind a wall of potted fruit trees to encourage him to forget I'm here.

"Rae?" Rob appears around a corner. "It looks like these azaleas are the way to go. Any objections?"

He sounds impatient. Behind him the salesclerk is waiting sweetly with a red wagon, ready to load up.

"What is it?" Rob says on the way home. He stares straight ahead. Behind us, the pink flowers fill the back seat like children. "What *is* it?"

"If you really wanted to know, you wouldn't ask like that."

"I *do* want to know. But when I asked you nicely, you said 'Nothing.'"

"But you knew it wasn't nothing and you let it go at that."

"I let it go because I knew you were upset and I didn't want to make it worse."

"See? That's what I mean. You knew something was wrong but you weren't willing to press it, to deal with it."

"Okay. I'm sorry. Whatever." Rob's voice suddenly goes even. He adjusts the rearview mirror. "I'm ready. I'm willing to deal with it. Let's talk about it now."

I look over at him. He's got the unruffled profile of a chauffeur. I hate myself for what I'm about to do, but I can't help it. "Forget it. I don't want to talk about it now." I watch his eyelids press closed for a long second.

Neither of us speaks the rest of the way. I try to think of something to say once we're home, silently unloading the cheerful, springy plants from the back seat, but nothing comes to me.

In the house, Rob goes to hang up his jacket and returns with a book he's been reading lately. Without looking in my direction, he deposits himself on the couch, a place neither of us ever sits during the day.

Without entirely meaning to, I cross the room and find my hand on the knob of the front door. "Well, I guess I'm going out. I'll be back in a couple hours."

"Where are you going?" Rob's voice is soft. He stands up, holding the book closed around his finger.

"I don't know, Robert." The door is open now. "I don't know where I'm going."

On the way to the car I am thinking, You should stay. You should go back inside and put your arms around him, lay your head at the base of his throat.

But I am also thinking, He should have put the book down. He should not have saved his place.

I throw the car in reverse and back it too fast out of the driveway, scraping the muffler against the curb.

---

I have nowhere to go, so I drive to Joann's. Her house cheers me up because children live there, and the available surfaces are always cluttered with a jumble of art projects, blue nail polish, library books on Costa Rica or Greenland, wind-up toys that somersault in the air.

Joann answers the door in sweat clothes. Her thick black hair, pulled back, is beginning to fight its way loose. She looks the way magazine advertisements would have you believe most women look when they are doing housework.

"Rae? Great, you're here," she says, rushing me into a hug.

"You can help me move the couch back. The kids said they would, but they're nowhere to be seen."

She leads me through the furniture-choked hallway to the empty living room, which is sending up the virtuous scent of rug shampoo. The last afternoon light is coming in through the big windows and the room looks huge, spotless, like a room in a dream. "Careful, no shoes yet," Joann says, so we enter in bare feet. The rug feels puffy, faintly damp. I am almost knocked down by a swift, keen urge to switch lives with her, to take morning coffee in this brand-new room and start over.

We move the couch into place and then head into the kitchen. With men, my important conversations have always been on highways, at night, the streetlights rhythmically flooding the car every few seconds and then returning it to darkness. But my best talks with women have always taken place at kitchen tables. Joann clears a stack of clothing catalogues and skateboarding magazines off a chair and motions for me to sit down. The phone begins to ring as she is getting down the wineglasses, and she pours us each a glass before answering it. I drink, exhale for what feels like the first time in an hour, and flip through a magazine called *Thrasher*.

"Oh, hi," Joann says, followed by a string of increasingly un-certain-sounding uh-huhs. "Look, Malcolm, let's just cut to the chase," she finally says in an impatient rush. "It's money, isn't it? We know that because it's always money. That's pretty much it, isn't it?"

The boys in the magazine are grimacing with concentration. In their crash helmets and protective pads, they look like young, de-termined soldiers.

"Malcolm, I'm not trying to make you *feel* guilty, you *are* guilty. These kids are your responsibility, too. It's not their fault you've got two new babies on your payroll."

Joann is turned around now, facing the appliances. She's wound the phone cord around herself a couple of times; the coils are pulled taut against her baggy sweatshirt.

After a pause she says wearily, almost tenderly, "Damn you, Malcolm. God damn you to hell." Then she untangles herself and carefully hangs up the phone and looks out the window at the weedy backyard. "Lord, I hate that man," she says, her back still to me. "I can't believe I ever thought I loved him enough to marry him. Why are we so stupid when we're young?"

We drink our wine. I don't feel like talking about my fight with Rob. Now that I'm out of the house, I don't want to think about it, so I focus on the wine and let Joann go on about the kids.

"Annie's going through some sort of phase. I get the feeling that everything I do embarrasses her. Sometimes I catch her looking at me and I can just feel her thinking, 'Whatever I do, I'm not ending up like her,' meaning me.

"And Nick has a new girlfriend." Joann frowns at her glass.

"Well, that's good," I say. The wine is starting to make me fuzzy. "Girlfriends are good."

"You should see this girl," Joann says. "She has breasts." And she holds her hands out in front of her chest in the sort of gesture I can imagine being popular with boys in junior high. "So I got up my nerve and I sat Nick down for"—she hooks her fingers in the air to put the next words in quotation marks—"'the talk.'"

"No, really," she says when I start to laugh. "You'd be surprised how hard it is to talk to your children about this stuff."

"So, what did you say?"

"I asked him if he and his father had talked about sex at all. He nodded in this vague way which I knew meant no, and then he gave me this look like he was trying to be very patient with me, and he said, 'How come parents think kids are thinking about sex all the time when it's the parents who are doing all the thinking about it?'"

"Ha!" I say. "That makes a lot of sense."

Joann shakes her head and says, "I thought it sounded like a *very* well rehearsed answer. Then he says to me, 'Don't worry, Mom. I know what I'm doing,' which is of course the signal to start worrying. And he comes over and gives me a kiss on the forehead."

I have been pacing myself against Joann's drinking. When she drains her second glass in a healthy swallow, I do the same. "That's sweet," I say. "That was a sweet thing for him to do."

"Rae," she says, levelly, putting her hand over mine, "sometimes it is so obvious you've never had kids it's frightening."

I can see the door to Nick's room from where I am sitting; it is covered with stickers celebrating brand names for wetsuits and sunglasses, a bumper sticker that reads "Skateboarding Is Not a Crime," and a ragged length of yellow tape bearing the legend "Police Line—Do Not Cross." It is completely closed and reminds me of the doors of my youth—doors I had slammed against my brother, then opened and slammed again if the first time had not been loud enough; doors that would not lock and had to be held closed against my sister's pushing strength; doors that did lock but could be finessed open with a kitchen knife; doors closed quietly, sighed shut, late at night, to keep from waking my parents. I have not closed a door any of these ways since I moved out of my parents' house; the thought makes me feel oddly lonely, alone.

"Still," I say. "They're your children. You love them. They give your life meaning."

"Rae, this isn't television here, this is real life," Joann says. She is looking me dead in the eye. "My children are the only thing in the world I would die for. I mean literally die for. That has its advantages and its disadvantages. It's a complicated situation."

When I get home, Rob is in the same spot on the couch, sitting with his book and his whiskey glass in a weak cone of lamplight. The rest of the room has gone dark. He looks up but he doesn't move.

"I went to Joann's," I volunteer. "Did you fix yourself something to eat?" I am working my way toward something, toward apologizing.

"Joann's? Is that what this is all about? That I paid too much attention to Joann at that party?"

I listen for a moment to all the spring night noises, the whirs and clicks. Something is making a racket out there.

I consider the possibilities.

"Because, number one, I wasn't, and number two, I was just trying to be nice because she's your friend and I know that's important to you. Rae? Oh, come on, Rae."

"No," I say. "No, that's not it."

He closes his eyes and kneads the bridge of his nose the way people who wear glasses sometimes do. But he does not wear glasses; this is a habit he has picked up from me.

"Well, okay then. All right," he says. "Good. Then let's hit the sack, then. Let's just go to bed."

---

"Rob? I think we should talk."

We are lying in bed, on our backs. He reaches for my hand. "Not now," he says. "In the morning." His voice is thick with sleep and whiskey.

I pull my hand away. "No, we should talk now. It's not good to go to sleep like this, all tense and everything. We should work it out." But he is already gone, asleep.

I listen angrily for a few minutes to the sound of my husband's easy, even breathing, and then I climb out of bed and go out into the living room.

When I was in high school, babysitting on the weekends, I used to sit by myself in other people's living rooms and try to imagine what their private lives were like. I didn't like to baby-sit—I was always afraid the children would fall or swallow something or die mysteriously in their beds—but my mother shamed me into accepting jobs by telling me how tired she used to get taking care of the four of us kids and how much it meant to her to be able to leave us in someone else's care for a few hours on a Friday or Saturday night. I'd be on the phone with some neighbor, trying to make up some excuse for why I wasn't available, and my mother would shoot me this look. She'd be on her way to the basement with her arms full of laundry, wearing a housecoat and her nurse's shoes, and I'd remember that I'd left my breakfast dishes on the table and I hadn't picked up my room, which she'd asked me to do, and I'd find myself saying yes, this Friday would be fine, what time should I be there?

I worked mostly for the Thomases, a young couple who lived down our street. He was an architect and, my best friend and I agreed, the handsomest man we knew personally. She had been a model before they got married, and she wore a lot of pearls and snug black dresses when they went out. They kept their radio tuned to the classical-music station, and at Christmas, when our tree looked like something on display at J. C. Penney, their tree was trimmed with tiny white lights and white satin bows. They called each other "darling," and I was convinced, based on a photograph on Mr. Thomas's dresser of a bare-shouldered Mrs. Thomas in bed, that they slept in the nude. Books were stacked and splayed throughout the house, and my general impression was that once the children were in bed, they read until they were overcome with desire for each other, made passionate love in whatever room they happened to be in, then fell, exhausted and satisfied, into the bed they shared, and slept in each other's embrace.

On the nights I babysat, they always told me to eat whatever was in the refrigerator that looked appealing and to feel free to watch the "idiot box," but the moment I heard their car turn in the driveway, I would click the television off and pretend to be reading or doing my homework. We would stand in the living room, talking quietly about their evening and the children. Mrs. Thomas would slip out of her shoes and pull off her earrings and Mr. Thomas would reach for his wallet and ask me what the damages were. He always rounded up to the nearest dollar in paying me, as though he found coins embarrassing. Then his wife would climb upstairs to check on the children and he would drive me home, the tiny sports car smelling of leather, cologne, and alcohol.

"The kids are crazy about you," he said one night as he pulled in front of my house, the tires squeaking against the curb. He had one of those soft voices that seemed to find its way to your ear and curl up there. Everything he said sounded like a secret.

"Well, I'm extremely fond of them," I said. I never seemed to sound like myself on these short trips home. "They're wonderful children."

I opened the door a crack and the interior light went on. "Well," I said. "Thank you for the ride. Good night, now."

But as I started to climb out, he turned the ignition off and the car fell silent. Instinctively, I froze in mid-exit, one foot already planted on the sidewalk.

"You're a very serious girl, aren't you, Rae?"

I was at an age where I did not often hear men other than my father say my name, and the sound of it felt like a warm hand on my thigh. I had no idea what to say, but I turned back toward him from my awkward perch on the edge of the seat and tried to ease my leg inconspicuously back into the car.

"You're just waiting for your life to start, aren't you?" he went on. "Waiting for the first remarkable event in that remarkable chain of remarkable events to happen, that destiny that you are destined for."

His side of the windshield was beginning to fog up. I knew he had been drinking, but I did believe those things about myself and I wanted to believe that he recognized them, too. This is it, I thought. This is how it starts. This is the beginning of my real life.

I had managed to get back into my seat, and as I pulled the door gently closed, the light abruptly went out. Mr. Thomas didn't say anything; he seemed not to have noticed. My heart began to pound loud enough, I was sure, to be heard. I slid my hands between my clamped knees and looked out the window at my house. It looked dimly familiar, a place I had once lived. I sat very still and waited for Mr. Thomas to say something more.

"Why do we think that, I wonder," he said finally. "Where do we get the idea that the world will know who we are?"

I took a long moment to absorb this. It made me feel embarrassed, as though I had been caught enjoying something dumb on television. But I was excited, too—by the darkness of the car, by the way the edge of his coat spilled onto my seat, by the word *we*. I stared at Mr. Thomas's hands, still on the steering wheel, and wished for something smart to say.

"You know," he said, clearing his throat, "a few months ago I went for four days without sleeping." He seemed to be talking to the speedometer. "I suddenly lost the ability to sleep. I wore one of those masks at night to keep my eyes closed so they wouldn't dry out, but I never lost consciousness. I thought something final and absolute was happening to me."

Out of the corner of my eye, I saw the light go on in my parents' bedroom.

"That was the strangest thing that ever happened to me. When it was over I thought how grateful I was to have a normal life again."

It was my turn to say something. "Life is certainly odd, isn't it?" I tried, uncomfortably. When he didn't respond, I began to feel self-conscious. It occurred to me that he was just waiting for me to get out of the car. "Well, I'd better be going inside," I said, feeling ridiculous now. "Thanks again for the ride."

"Rae?"

I turned toward him again, and this time he was looking right at me. His face began to close in on mine and when I didn't pull away, he tilted his head slightly to the side and kissed me on the mouth. He still had one hand on the steering wheel, but the other was now resting on the top of the seat near my head. My hands were in my jacket pockets, closed in fists around my house key and my babysitting money. He kissed me again and I gave a little back this time, pressing my nose into his rough cheek. He pulled away and smiled at me. I found the door handle again after a furtive search, and concentrated on climbing out of the low seat as gracefully as I could manage.

My mother was sitting at the kitchen table when I came in. She was in her robe and slippers, drinking a cup of hot milk.

"What are you doing up?" I said, sure she knew everything.

"Nothing. Thinking. How did it go tonight?"

My mother was always curious to know where the Thomases had spent their evening and what Mrs. Thomas had worn.

I did not want to get into it. "To a friend's, I think."

"I wish we would go out more. I wish I could get your father to do things like that."

I did not want to get into this, either. "Well, I think I'll head up to bed," I said. "Are you coming?"

"In a minute," she said. I leaned down and kissed her good night. She smelled like sleep and warm milk, like a kid.

---

In the kitchen I wrap myself in the afghan and listen to one of the call-in shows on the radio. The woman psychiatrist, Dr. Brenner, is hosting it. She has a good voice for the job—compassionate and professional at the same time—and she leans toward compromise and conciliation in her advice. The station's other psychiatrist, Dr. Max, is the hard-liner, the bad cop. "What I hear you saying," he'll say, "is that you know your wife's having an affair and you're choosing to deny it instead of cope with it. My advice to you, if your wife's behavior bothers you, and it certainly sounds like it does, is to confront her with it."

In Dr. Brenner's more forgiving view, there's a lot of stress out there and most of us don't get enough rest and quiet time together. We don't eat right. We watch too much violent TV and we've never recovered, as a culture, from Bo Derek.

I get up to get myself a glass of milk and notice in the sink a plastic container with a fork in it, collecting water under the dripping faucet. Rob has been studying chaos theory recently, a set of ideas that describe things that move without linear pattern, a way of explaining things we know will happen but can't predict. When the next drip will fall from a leaky spigot. Heart attacks. Earthquakes. Civil wars.

I watch the tiny splash each drip makes and think of my husband, hours earlier, pacing the kitchen in the approaching darkness, eating a cold, leftover dinner standing up, not bothering with a napkin or plate. I think of him listening for the sound of the car in the driveway, the faint squeak of the front door being opened, the blurred, vague sounds of weight moving through space that tell you someone is in the next room. I think of him waiting with nervous patience for the most predictable, inexplicable thing to happen—for his wife to come home.

On the radio the doctor urges a woman to let go of the grudge she holds against her sister for stealing her boyfriend away and then counsels a man to invite his estranged son over for dinner. *My God*, the voice says. *He's your son. What are you waiting for?*

And I stand at the sink, trembling, afraid and grateful that this is all there is.

*The Iowa Short Fiction Award and John Simmons Short Fiction Award Winners*

**1998**
*The River of Lost Voices,*
Mark Brazaitis
Judge: Stuart Dybek

**1998**
*Friendly Fire,*
Kathryn Chetkovich
Judge: Stuart Dybek

**1997**
*Thank You for Being Concerned and Sensitive,* Jim Henry
Judge: Ann Beattie

**1997**
*Within the Lighted City,*
Lisa Lenzo
Judge: Ann Beattie

**1996**
*Hints of His Mortality,*
David Borofka
Judge: Oscar Hijuelos

**1996**
*Western Electric,* Don Zancanella
Judge: Oscar Hijuelos

**1995**
*Listening to Mozart,*
Charles Wyatt
Judge: Ethan Canin

**1995**
*May You Live in Interesting Times,* Tereze Glück
Judge: Ethan Canin

**1994**
*The Good Doctor,*
Susan Onthank Mates
Judge: Joy Williams

**1994**
*Igloo among Palms,*
Rod Val Moore
Judge: Joy Williams

**1993**
*Happiness,* Ann Harleman
Judge: Francine Prose

**1993**
*Macauley's Thumb,*
Lex Williford
Judge: Francine Prose

**1993**
*Where Love Leaves Us,*
Renée Manfredi
Judge: Francine Prose

**1992**
*My Body to You,*
Elizabeth Searle
Judge: James Salter

**1992**
*Imaginary Men,* Enid Shomer
Judge: James Salter

**1991**
*The Ant Generator,*
Elizabeth Harris
Judge: Marilynne Robinson

**1991**
*Traps,* Sondra Spatt Olsen
Judge: Marilynne Robinson

1990
*A Hole in the Language,*
Marly Swick
Judge: Jayne Anne Phillips

1989
*Lent: The Slow Fast,*
Starkey Flythe, Jr.
Judge: Gail Godwin

1989
*Line of Fall,* Miles Wilson
Judge: Gail Godwin

1988
*The Long White,*
Sharon Dilworth
Judge: Robert Stone

1988
*The Venus Tree,*
Michael Pritchett
Judge: Robert Stone

1987
*Fruit of the Month,* Abby Frucht
Judge: Alison Lurie

1987
*Star Game,* Lucia Nevai
Judge: Alison Lurie

1986
*Eminent Domain,* Dan O'Brien
Judge: Iowa Writers' Workshop

1986
*Resurrectionists,*
Russell Working
Judge: Tobias Wolff

1985
*Dancing in the Movies,*
Robert Boswell
Judge: Tim O'Brien

1984
*Old Wives' Tales,*
Susan M. Dodd
Judge: Frederick Busch

1983
*Heart Failure,* Ivy Goodman
Judge: Alice Adams

1982
*Shiny Objects,* Dianne Benedict
Judge: Raymond Carver

1981
*The Phototropic Woman,*
Annabel Thomas
Judge: Doris Grumbach

1980
*Impossible Appetites,*
James Fetler
Judge: Francine du Plessix Gray

1979
*Fly Away Home,* Mary Hedin
Judge: John Gardner

1978
*A Nest of Hooks,* Lon Otto
Judge: Stanley Elkin

1977
*The Women in the Mirror,*
Pat Carr
Judge: Leonard Michaels

1976
*The Black Velvet Girl,*
C. E. Poverman
Judge: Donald Barthelme

1975
*Harry Belten and the*
*Mendelssohn Violin Concerto,*
Barry Targan
Judge: George P. Garrett

1974
*After the First Death There Is No Other*, Natalie L. M. Petesch
Judge: William H. Gass

1973
*The Itinerary of Beggars*,
H. E. Francis
Judge: John Hawkes

1972
*The Burning and Other Stories*,
Jack Cady
Judge: Joyce Carol Oates

1971
*Old Morals, Small Continents, Darker Times*,
Philip F. O'Connor
Judge: George P. Elliott

1970
*The Beach Umbrella*,
Cyrus Colter
Judges: Vance Bourjaily and Kurt Vonnegut, Jr.

Photo credit: Jude Todd

Kathryn Chetkovich has spent most of her
life in California and currently makes
her home in the Santa Cruz Mountains.
Her stories have appeared in the *Georgia
Review, New England Review, Mississippi Review,* and ZYZZYVA.